Throne
of
Deceit

Dragons of Isentol Book 1

RICHARD FIERCE

PDMAC

Dragonfire Press

Copyright © 2020 Richard Fierce

Cover design by germancreative.

Cover art by Rosauro Ugang

ISBN: 978-1-947329-43-0

CONTENTS

THANK YOU

To our wives, with all our hearts.

CHAPTER 1

Gwen

The Seven Stars inn was busier than normal.

That was good for business, but it also meant that Gwen had been rushing around most of the evening, filling tankards and delivering steaming food. It was warm, uncomfortably so, and Gwen was glad the night was almost over. The air was thick with pipe smoke and boisterous laughter, a rarity these days.

Gwen spotted a man waving his arm, tankard upside down on the table. She heaved a weary sigh and hurried to the table, forcing a smile.

"More ale?" she asked.

"Yes, and keep it flowing," the man replied.

Gwen could tell by the way he slurred his words that he'd probably already had too much, but she nodded and refilled his tankard. The inn would be closing soon, so not much more ale would be "flowing" anyway. Gwen's father had been in the kitchen since opening, fulfilling the endless stream of orders and cursing when he burned himself, which was quite often.

A bard began playing a cheerful song, his fingers flying over the strings of his lute with a practiced ease. Gwen liked the melodies he played, but he was passing through and tonight would be his last performance at the inn. She did another loop of the tables, making sure the patrons were taken care of, then sat behind the bar and listened to the music.

Gwen found the bard handsome. He was young and energetic, his face clean shaven, and his brown hair trimmed short and neat. Her father would never allow her to marry someone with a profession that required constant travel, but she didn't see any problem with admiring the man's attractiveness. Besides that, it was common knowledge that Gwen would take over the Seven Stars once her father retired.

As the bard finished his song, a commotion outside the inn caught Gwen's attention. She looked to the windows, but it was too dark to see anything other than vague shadows. The noise drew the attention of the inn's customers as well, and the people quickly congregated in front of the windows. Those who couldn't squeeze in among the others exited the doors to see things up close.

Gwen heard angry shouting and groaned. Drunken men fist fighting one another wasn't uncommon, especially when the place was busy. She removed her apron and hung it on one of the hooks on the wall, then walked to the door and cracked it open, peering out into the night.

A single man was surrounded by a group of the king's soldiers. Their black leather armor made them blend in with the darkness, but Gwen knew the attire. The soldiers had become a common sight around the inn, and around Dawsbury in general. Rumors of war had been circulating for years, but now there were signs of it. Aside from the presence of the king's men, there were also whispers of dark magic and sightings of dragons.

Gwen didn't know what to think about any of it. She lived a simple life working at the inn, and she wanted it to stay that way. The king could make war on the surrounding kingdoms if he wanted to, so long as Gwen's way of life wasn't impacted. Her attention was jerked back to the present when one of the soldiers kicked the back of the man's legs, knocking him to the ground. The man being harassed scowled and tried to get back up.

"Stay down, dog," one of the soldiers said.

"Yeah," chimed in another. "If you know what's good for you."

Someone bumped into Gwen from behind and she looked over her shoulder to see Tobias, the baker's son.

"What's going on out there?" he asked.

"Some of the soldiers have taken an interest in Garre," Gwen replied. "Garre's angry, but I think he'll keep his temper under control."

"I can't stand those soldiers," Tobias muttered. "They think they can come to our town and do whatever they want just because they wear the king's emblem."

"As long as we stay out of their way, we don't have anything to worry about," Gwen said. "They're just following orders."

Tobias snorted but didn't say anything.

Garre was glaring daggers at the soldiers, but he stayed where he was.

"Good dog," one of the soldiers goaded. "Now lick the dirt off my boots."

"Screw off," Garre spat.

The soldier who'd spoke drew his sword and

leveled the tip at Garre's throat. "What was that, dog? Did I tell you to speak?"

Silence fell over everyone in the inn. Gwen watched intently, her heart hammering in her chest with anxiety. "They can't kill someone for no reason," she whispered.

"That's what you'd think, anyway," Tobias said. "When left unchecked, that tyrant's hired hands will do anything, including murdering innocent people."

"Watch your words, boy," one of the patrons said. "You'll bring the king's wrath down on us all."

Gwen watched with bated breath, silently praying that Garre wouldn't be hurt. She wasn't friends with him, but she knew who he was, and they'd never had any issues. Even if they had, Gwen would never wish harm on anyone.

"Get to licking," the soldier demanded, lifting his boot near Garre's face. For a moment, Gwen thought he was going to lick the soldier's boot. Instead, Garre grabbed onto the soldier's leg and pulled, forcing the soldier to fall onto his back.

"Yeah!" Tobias shouted. "Give him what for!"

Gwen had a feeling something terrible was about to happen. The soldier scrambled back onto his feet and kicked Garre in the face. Garre crumbled backward awkwardly, his legs tucked under his body.

"Gods," Gwen said, flinching and looking at Tobias.

"Someone has to do something," Tobias said. "They're going to kill him."

"Don't say that," Gwen replied.

Tobias stared at her, jaw clenched. "No more," he said.

Before Gwen could figure out what he meant, Tobias drew a dagger and pushed past her. He sprinted toward the soldier that had kicked Garre and leaped onto his back, driving the small blade into the soldier's chest.

The world froze.

Gwen's eyes widened in horror and surprise. She screamed, and the world began moving again, but now it was a blur. The other soldiers grabbed Tobias and forced him to the ground, wrenching his dagger away. The soldier he'd attempted to stab was uninjured.

"Some dogs don't understand loyalty," he said, then lifted his sword up threateningly. With a sudden grunt, he staggered forward as Garre pushed him from behind. Another soldier drew his sword and thrust it into Garre's back.

Gwen stepped back from the door, shaken. Garre screamed and fell to the ground, writhing in the dirt. There was confusion among the rest of the soldiers as they glanced at each other with uncertainty. Tobias broke free of the men holding him and sprinted to the left, running down the alley beside the inn.

The apparent leader threw his arms up. "Don't just stand there, get him!"

The others chased after Tobias and Gwen quietly shut the door and returned to the bar. The patrons slowly went back to their tables, but the mood had changed. The bard had stopped playing his music and the conversations became muted.

Gwen wrung her hands together nervously, not knowing what she could do to help Garre. Should she help him? What if he had done something to warrant the interest of the soldiers and she wasn't privy to that knowledge? She started to head around the bar when the kitchen door flung open and Tobias ran in, followed by Boris, Gwen's father.

"What's going on?" Boris demanded.

"I need somewhere to hide," Tobias replied. He looked around the inn, frantic. Gwen thought he looked like a frightened deer, ready to flee at any moment.

Boris looked around the room, noting the patrons, then grabbed onto the edge of the bar. "Help me, will you?"

Tobias grabbed the other end and, together, they heaved the stout wooden structure forward. Gwen was surprised to see a trap door hidden in the floor.

Boris opened the small door and motioned to the darkness within. "Go," he said. "Hurry."

Tobias didn't question the order and hurried down into the hidden space. Boris closed the door and tried to move the bar back into place, but it was too heavy. He looked at Gwen, then changed his mind and turned to the customers.

"Someone give me a hand!"

A few people leaped to their feet to help and, within a few moments, the bar was back in place.

"Father," Gwen said softly, following him into the kitchen. "You never told me about that door."

"Forget that you ever saw it," Boris replied, washing his hands off in a bucket of clean water. He went back to preparing meals as if nothing had happened.

Gwen watched her father work, wondering why his demeanor had changed so suddenly. There was something he wasn't telling her, that much was obvious. There was shouting in the common room and Gwen rushed out of the kitchen. The soldiers had entered the inn and were harassing the customers.

"Gentlemen," Gwen greeted loudly, offering the largest smile she could muster. "Drinks?"

"We're looking for a criminal," one of them said. Gwen turned her attention to him and recognized him as the leader of the group from outside.

"I don't think I've seen anyone shady in here, but I'll help if I can," Gwen said cheerily. She was surprised her voice hadn't cracked.

"This person is an enemy of the king. He's dangerous and we need to remove him from the streets. He's about my height and build, with black hair."

Gwen put a puzzled look on her face and slowly shook her head. "I can't say I've seen anyone like that in here. Would you like a drink while your men ask my customers?"

"I'd love one, but I must refuse. I'm on duty."

"Right. Can't have you out there staggering around on the job." Gwen laughed. The soldier didn't share her mirth. The kitchen door opened as Boris came out, carrying a tray full of food. The soldier jumped, obviously startled, then calmed when he saw there was no threat.

"Evening," Boris greeted as he passed them,

delivering the food to a table by the windows.

"If you see anyone matching the description, please report it to the local constabulary. They'll get word to us."

"I will," Gwen replied.

The soldier turned his back to Gwen, and she noticed the uneasiness of the customers. Most were minding their own business, but a few people were staring death at the soldiers. Boris returned to the bar and the lead soldier stopped him.

"Are you the owner?"

"I am," Boris replied, offering a grin. "It's a humble place, but it's served me well."

"It's a dump," the soldier grunted. "I've also heard that it's a den of protection for the king's enemies."

Boris looked pained. "I hope no one questions my devotion to the king," he said. "I've been a staunch supporter all my years."

The soldier stared at Boris intently, then nodded, seeming satisfied.

"Anything?" the soldier asked his men.

"Nothing," someone answered.

"Let's go, then." The lead soldier looked from Boris to Gwen, then headed for the door. His men followed after him and they exited the inn. Gwen sighed in relief and leaned over the bar.

"That was close," she whispered.

There was a pounding noise at the door and Gwen realized that the soldiers were securing it so that no one could leave.

"Father, what's happening? Why did he say we're hiding enemies here?"

Boris suddenly looked older to her. Deep lines spread across his face and there were bags under his eyes.

"There are things I haven't told you because I wanted to keep you safe," Boris replied.

The customers of the inn began to panic and started kicking at the door. A few others picked up chairs and broke some of the windows, but they were greeted with flaming torches that were thrown into the inn. People scattered out of the way, knocking over tables and spilling drinks. Alcohol hit the torches and flames spread across the floor.

"We've got to get out of here!" Gwen shouted.

Boris grabbed her hand and led her through the kitchen to the backdoor, but when he pushed on it, it didn't budge.

"They've blocked us in," Boris said grimly.

CHAPTER 2

Conal

Shackled to the thick iron rings hammered into the granite walls in a dank prison was not the outcome Conal had in mind when he agreed to lead the latest raid on the market city. Once again he berated himself for ignoring his gut feeling.

"It'll be easy," Oscon had said. "A walk in the park. Get in, get out and by the time yer back here they won't know what happened."

"Why me?" Conal frowned at the bandit chief, a hulking lummox of a man, beetle browed with a sneer for a smile.

"'cause nobody'd expect you. Ya got that baby-face look like yer a choirboy."

Conal's first instinct was to ask him the real reason for this sudden elevation to lead a raid. Until then, he had been little more than a gopher or a lookout. It wasn't until he overheard Oscon talking about moving on because they had pretty much skimmed all they could from the area towns and cities and the constabulary and soldier patrols were becoming too frequent that caused Conal to wonder why do another raid? When he heard Oscon talk about thinning his herd, he knew something wasn't right.

But vanity overruled his misgivings, and when Oscon poked a thick finger at him and said, "Yer gonna lead this one," Conal had squashed his reservations and stepped forward. His uneasiness was somewhat allayed when Oscon selected a few of the best men and women to go along.

The setup played out to perfection.

Once in the town, Conal had been recognized and immediately surrounded by four guards and four swords pointed much too closely at various parts of his body. When Conal frantically looked for help, there was none. The six men and women who had so assiduously listened to his plan and followed him into town had melted away like morning dew. Had Conal paid more attention to his followers, he might have noticed them disappearing one by one that by the time he was in the market center by the tax boxes, he was quite alone.

The ultimate insult was when he swore the voice calling out, "I know him. He's a bandit," belonged to his second in command, Jestyn.

And now here he sat amidst the overlapping stench of unwashed bodies and the layered decay of the dead, wondering why Oscon had decided he was no longer useful, and vowing that he would hunt him down if it was the last thing he ever did, which by the look of things might be a tad difficult.

His broodings were interrupted when he heard the far cell door grind open and a nobly dressed man, flanked by several guards eased his way through the cell, holding a handkerchief at his nose and mouth. Conal watched as the man occasionally stopped and pointed whereupon two guards would grab the prisoner, unshackle him or her before handcuffing them and leading them away.

When the man stopped in front of him, Conal flashed a loopy smile and received a pointed finger in return whereupon he was yanked up, unshackled and handcuffed, and led through the squalid mass of bodies, out through the door and recesses of the prison keep to finally emerge into the mid-morning outside and fresh air.

Conal inhaled a deep satisfying breath then glanced to his left and right at the other prisoners lined up on both sides of him. There were ten of them, six women and four men, all young and healthy, all handcuffed.

The sergeant of the guard stood imperiously before them. He was a toad of a man, all body and skinny legs wrapped in an ill-fitting uniform of the town's constabulary: crimson jacket with gold buttons, straight tan cotton trousers tucked into calf-high boots, and a leather helmet capped with a bristle that looked like someone had lost a shoe brush.

Behind him the noble man stood, aloof bordering on ennui, the handkerchief still at his mouth. He wore a long-sleeved white silk shirt, covered by a white cream-colored vest of the finest calfskin. His ebony trousers were handcrafted from rabbit skin, and his boots a work of art in reptile skin. He eschewed a hat and his full-bodied blond hair fell about his shoulders, framing a handsome face with square jaw and dark brown eyes. Conal guessed him to be closing in on 40.

"In accordance with Kingdom Statute 43 dash 12," the sergeant bellowed, reading from an unfurled parchment, "and with the honest and whole-hearted concurrence of the Burgomaster of Hemlyn, you have been redeemed by Lord Pharyl.

Your death sentences have been commuted to a life of servitude until such time that you die or are provided your freedom according to the wishes of Lord Pharyl, Prince of the realm of Vandyr. You are henceforth to be branded so that all may know the depths to which you have fallen. Should you choose to escape, know that you are subject to the laws of exile and retribution. Anyone finding an escaped slave may kill him or her."

Pharyl. Conal knew the name. The man ruled this part of the kingdom with an iron fist inside a velvet glove. He could be as cruel as he was generous. Conal felt a flash of relief, knowing he would stay alive if he played his cards right. Those poor fettered souls left behind in the prison were as good as dead.

Rolling up the parchment, the sergeant nodded to the guards who force-marched the newly anointed slaves to the center of town so that the entire populace could witness their debasement. Men, women, and curious children stood in a thick circle around the branding pit, the heat from the fire keeping them back while providing enough space for the guards to hold the victim down for the Branding Master who instructed the poor soul to stay as still as possible,. Moving while being branded caused a bad brand, requiring a second one. The normal location of a slave brand, concentric circles the size of a large coin, was on the cheek.

Despite the rising fear of having his face forever marred, Conal noticed there were four irons in the fire. He knew the reason. Some slaves had a different brand placed on the outside of the right shoulder – the death's head, a skull with horns. These slaves were bound to protect the master with their lives. Two other branding irons consisted of a viper and a rose.

The viper brand was placed on the upper left arm. Vipers were the master's enforcers, assassins, and muscle. They lived well and it was considered an honor to be a viper, for vipers could marry and the children of the marriage were considered freeborn.

The rose brand was placed on the right thigh. A rose slave was a pleasure slave. Conal prayed to whatever god or gods were out there that he would not be a rose slave, for he knew what happened to rose slaves. Sure, there were the few who had pleased their masters and allowed to live a life of privilege in the harem. But the majority of rose slaves, those whose beauty had faded, were sent to the farms to spend the rest of their lives in back-breaking labor.

The fourth iron? Conal frowned in puzzlement for only a moment until his attention was diverted by Lord Pharyl who causally strolled down the line to stand in front of the first person, an attractive blond woman about Conal's age.

Staring at the woman for only a moment, Pharyl dipped a finger at her. "Rose."

As the woman was dragged off to be branded, Pharyl side-stepped to the next slave, a tall strong teenager. "Death's Head."

Conal was seventh in line and his prayers increased in urgency and pleading as Pharyl continued down the line, announcing, "Rose."

"Death's Head." "Rose." "Rose."

Pharyl stopped to appraise Conal as though he were judging a good horse. Folding his arms, he scrutinized the young man, impressed that the slave didn't avert his eyes or appear to grovel. Instead the young man stood firm, appearing to be unafraid.

"Either you're a sheep who has no clue of what's going to happen, or you've resigned yourself to fate. Which is it?"

"Fate, m'Lord."

"You answer with a strong voice," Pharyl said with a slow nod, noting the young man didn't call him master as was required. "Men like you tend to be wild, like a stallion that needs to be broken. They're too high-spirited. Are you high-spirited?"

Conal smiled at him. "It all depends upon the rider, m'Lord. A skilled rider knows his mount, knows how to direct and coax with just the right words. A gifted rider and mount are a team to be envied."

A smile flitted across Pharyl's lips. "You talk as one educated. Are you educated?"

"Yes, m'Lord."

"Where was the failure then that you end up like this?" Pharyl looked down his nose at him.

Conal shrugged. "Bad crowd, bad choices. Not everyone who calls you friend is one."

"Well spoken," Pharyl acknowledged. "You're too pretty to have your cheek branded, and you're not big or strong enough to be a Death's Head."

Conal's hopes took a nosedive, especially with the "too pretty" comment. What was it with these people and his looks? There were plenty of men who were better looking. Why couldn't people see that he was smart, that he had a brain? Steeling himself for the inevitable and already dreaming of a way to escape, he was startled when Pharyl gently pushed a finger into his chest.

"Viper."

Without thinking, Conal did a fist pump and exclaimed, "Yes," causing Pharyl to smirk and flash a bemused glance at this curious fellow. He started to sidestep to the next one in line when he stopped at turned back to Conal.

"What is your name?"

"Conal, m'Lord."

Pharyl nodded and continued, the next three all designated a "rose." With the choices decided, Lord Pharyl stepped away to watch the branding, noting the demeanor of each slave. Amidst all the shifting and squirming and fear, only Conal seemed unaffected. In fact, the man seemed more than ready to get branded.

After the woman before Conal had the rose mark burned into her skin and went sniveling to the medicine tent, Conal marched up, sat down and pulled off his shirt, revealing a wiry and strong body, which elicited some whistles and catcalls, causing him to scowl. Bracing himself for the pain, he clenched his jaw, determined not to show weakness.

"Hold," Lord Pharyl commanded as the Brand Master withdrew the glowing red-hot Viper iron. He pointed to another iron next to it. "Use that one."

Suddenly fearing Lord Pharyl had changed his mind, Conal struggled to determine which iron held the rose brand. His anxiety elevated as his gaze narrowed on the Brand Master carefully retrieving the branding iron then approached him. The head was small like a rose, yet the design was wrong, and he frowned, twisting his head to glance up to Lord Pharyl.

"The cobra," Lord Pharyl calmly answered. "Do not disappoint me." He turned and walked away, the guard sergeant hustling up next to him, obsequiously nodding and agreeing with the lord's softly spoken conversation.

The Cobra.

Conal's fear morphed to confident elation as he watched the not so subtle change in the crowd. Some were immediately intimidated, others unsure, and still others scoffed that so inexperienced a man should be chosen as a Cobra. Yet they knew the reputation. The Cobra was a leader among assassins, the silent unseen killers. Still, a sense of relief spread through the crowd for they knew this man would be taken away from here, for he was known.

Conal flinched then strained to remain immobile as the hot iron burned his flesh, the smell of burnt skin and the pain on his arm causing tears to well up in his eyes. Yet he sat rooted like a statue, grimly enduring the suffering.

Finally, the Brand Master pulled the iron away and surveyed his work. "Looks good. A good image." He dipped his head in admiration. "You sat very still. Go to the tent for them to bandage your arm."

Conal was halfway to the tent when he heard the

screech of the next victim, a woman given a rose brand. Inside the tent, three healers applied salve and bandages to the branded areas. All too soon, the ten slaves were again in line, no handcuffs this time. The crowds had drifted away, and few remained to witness their departure.

Lord Pharyl sat astride a magnificent dappled stallion at least 17 hands high. He waited as the slaves were loaded into carts, leaning forward when Conal made ready to grab the wagon rail and climb aboard.

"You, young Conal."

Conal lowered his leg and turned to face his new master. "Yes, m'Lord."

"Do you ride?"

"Yes, m' Lord."

Pharyl nodded and flicked two fingers at his travel steward, a tall lean man with close cropped hair and beard. A few moments later, a servant led a sorrel mount almost as tall as Lord Pharyl's steed to stand next to the Lord and Master.

Pharyl narrowed his focus on Conal. "You will ride with me."

"Yes, m'Lord."

With practiced ease, Conal swung up into the saddle, took hold of the reigns and slipped his feet into the stirrups.

"We are ready, m'Lord," the steward announced.

"Then let's get started. I want to be in Denhelm by dinner time."

"Yes, m'Lord."

The steward bustled up to the first wagon and

climbed aboard, ticking his head at the driver who flicked the reins causing the wagon to lurch forward. Soon, four wagons containing nine slaves and supplies surrounded by a dozen men at arms, their Lord and Master and the newest Cobra plodded out of the city. Conal rode next to Pharyl who remained silent until they were out of the earshot of the city walls.

"It's a three-day ride to my castle," Pharyl spoke. "We have plenty of time to get acquainted. You will tell me everything there is to know about you, and I will tell you what I expect of you."

"Yes, m'Lord."

"You may perhaps wonder why I chose you to be a Cobra when you have so little experience."

"The thought did occur to me, m'Lord."

"I have an eye for talent, and I believe you have the gifts I require. Do not worry, you will be trained as required for a Cobra. You perform well for me and I will consider giving you your freedom."

Conal reverently tipped his head. "It will be an honor to serve you, m'Lord."

"Yes, I know," he replied with an indifferent nod. They loped along in silence for a bit. "Tell me, young Conal, what is the first thing you wish to do as a Cobra?"

Conal didn't have to think about the answer. "Find a certain outlaw… and make him rue the day he was born."

Pharyl chuckled. "All in good time, my young friend, all in good time."

CHAPTER 3

Gwen

Gwen digested Boris's words and realized that they were likely going to die.

"What about the trap door? Where does it lead?"

Boris grabbed a long knife from a stack of cutlery and led Gwen back into the common room. The customers had put the fires out, but the soldiers were still outside. He surveyed the damage and shook his head.

"There's a few things you should know, but now is not the time. If we get out of this alive, I promise I'll tell you everything. For now, know that the trap door is one of a few entrances into an underground tunnel that leads to the cemetery."

"That's outside the city," Gwen said.

"Exactly," Boris replied. "It's an escape route."

"An escape from what?"

Boris looked at the soldiers waiting outside, and Gwen followed his gaze.

"Why would we need to flee the king's soldiers? They're supposed to protect us. None of this makes any sense."

"Gents, someone help me. The rest of you, block the windows so those brutes can't see what we're doing."

The patrons lined up, shoulder to shoulder, and blocked the windows. One large man helped Boris push the bar forward, and Gwen marveled again at the fact that she'd never known the door was there.

Boris pulled it open, then took one of the lanterns off the wall and handed it to Gwen.

"At the bottom of the ladder you'll see two tunnels. One is a decoy and leads to a pitfall. Follow the tunnel on the right. It's a bit of a trek, but just keep going until you reach the stone door."

"You aren't coming with me?" Gwen asked.

"I'm afraid not," Boris answered. He wrapped Gwen in his arms and hugged her close, holding her for a long moment in silence. When he released her, he smiled at her and tucked some stray hairs behind her left ear. "Find Tobias when you get out of the tunnel. He'll keep you safe."

"I don't want to leave you," Gwen whispered. Her eyes welled and a tear slid down her cheek.

"Don't worry about me, girl. I've still got plenty of fight in these old bones. Those soldiers won't kill me so easily. Keep your tears for the grief that is sure to come in the future. Now go."

Gwen clenched her jaw against the sadness and nodded. She held onto the lantern and climbed down the ladder. She heard Boris ask if anyone else wanted to leave, and three people joined her in the tunnel. Then the trap door closed and the world went dark except for the dim light of the lantern.

She lifted it, shining the light in an arcing motion, and saw the two tunnels. "This way," she said, leading the others along the one to the right. Wooden beams were spaced every few feet, lining the walls and the ceiling overhead. Gwen wondered if her father had been involved in digging the tunnels, or if he had discovered them. Considering the events of the night, something told her it was the former.

They walked for what seemed like an eternity before Gwen noticed the ground began to slope upward. After another fifty feet, the lantern illuminated an archway. The stone door Boris had mentioned was partially open. Gwen pushed on it, forcing it fully open and stepped out into the night. The others followed her, then left the cemetery and headed for the road.

Boris had told her to find Tobias, but how did he expect her to do that? She had no idea where he might have gone. Besides that, he was a wanted man now. How could someone considered an enemy of the king keep her safe? Tobias would have his hands full evading the authorities. She sighed in frustration, facing more questions than answers.

Gwen glanced around the cemetery. There were tombstones scattered everywhere, but they were lined in an orderly fashion. A crypt towered over the rest of the graves, its white marble walls shining eerily under the light of the moon. Perched atop the roof were several gargoyles, their stone maws open in silent roars. Moss had overtaken their bodies, covering them in a thick green blanket.

The sound of approaching horses filled the air. Gwen killed the lantern, hid behind a tall headstone, and waited. As the horses drew closer, Gwen peeked out and saw it was more of the king's soldiers. They were heading toward Dawsbury. Gwen assumed that word must have reached the outpost and these soldiers were reinforcements. She waited until the horses were gone before stepping back into the open.

"Where do I go?" she whispered. It was hard for her to fathom how quickly her world of comfort had been ripped away.

A stick snapped nearby and her heart leaped within her chest. Before she could hide, a figure stepped into view wielding a sword. Gwen turned to run and slipped, falling and scraping her right knee on some rocks. She heard the figure running at her and screamed. A warm, sweaty hand clamped over her mouth.

"Quiet!"

Gwen knew the voice. She slapped the hand away and turned to look at Tobias. "You scared me!"

"I didn't mean to. I thought you were one of the king's soldiers. They're crawling all over Dawsbury."

"I wonder why," Gwen snapped. "You tried to stab one of them!"

"Keep your voice down," Tobias said. "What are you doing out here?"

"My father sent me. The soldiers locked everyone in the inn, accusing my father of hiding the king's enemies."

"Word finally got out," Tobias muttered. "I suppose it was only a matter of time."

"What are you talking about?"

"I know everything. You don't have to put on an act now."

"What act?" Gwen asked. "I have no idea what's happening!"

Tobias stared at her for a moment, then started

laughing. "Gods! He didn't tell you, did he?"

"Tell me what?"

"It makes sense, though. He was probably trying to protect you, but he should have told you what he was involved with."

"Stop talking to yourself and answer my question. What didn't my father tell me?" Gwen demanded.

Tobias sheathed his sword and closed the tomb door Gwen had come out of. "There's a war brewing."

"People have been saying that for years," Gwen said.

"This is different. I'm not sure what rock you've been under, but the king is not a good man. He's the source of most of our problems."

"What does that have to do with my father?"

"Boris has been helping the rebellion since it started. After his wife died, he put everything he had into the Seven Stars, but the king has raised our taxes so high that Boris lost ownership of the inn last year."

"He lost ownership of the inn?" Gwen closed her eyes and sighed. "Why didn't he tell me?"

"Maybe he thought he'd lose you, too? It's hard to say. The death of his wife was hard on him."

"Yes, I know. My mother's death was hard on us both."

Tobias went quiet, but the look on his face told Gwen he wanted to say something.

"What is it?" Gwen asked.

"It sounds like Boris told you less than I thought. Isabelle …"

"What about her?"

"She wasn't your mother," Tobias said. "And Boris isn't your father."

"Why would you say something like that? That's just hurtful."

"I'm being honest, Gwen. You were an orphan. Boris and Isabelle raised you like their own, but you were never in Isabelle's womb. Why do you think you're an only child? Isabelle was barren."

Gwen couldn't believe it. Tobias was making up outlandish tales at a time like this? Did he take her for a fool? She turned away from him and started for the road.

"Where are you going?"

"Away from you," Gwen replied.

"Gwen, wait. What *did* Boris tell you? Surely he said something before sending you out here?"

"He told me to find you and that you would keep me safe. He must have been overwhelmed when he said it, because he was clearly wrong about you."

"So, it's time then? We're not ready, but what choice do we have?"

Gwen paused. "Not ready for what?"

"To overthrow the king," Tobias said. "That's what Boris has been helping with. This tunnel has ferried more than people through it. We've been stockpiling weapons and other goods for months now."

"You're insane," Gwen blurted, tossing her hands into the air.

Another group of men were approaching. The galloping of their horses echoed off the headstones with an odd drum-like sound. Gwen dropped to all fours, and Tobias crawled over to her.

"We need to get moving," he whispered. "Boris wasn't wrong about me. I *can* keep you safe, but you're going to have to trust me."

"Why should I? You tried to kill a soldier."

"For good reason," Tobias replied. "Would you rather have let them kill Garre with no intervention?"

"Does it matter? Garre's dead now anyway."

Tobias groaned. "You're missing the point, Gwen. If we continue to let the king stomp on us, nothing will ever change. But if we stand up for ourselves and fight back, we can force change."

Gwen heard the passion behind his words and considered what he said with more seriousness. If her father had truly been aiding a rebellion, there was a reason for it. Tobias said the king was depraved. Added onto the knowledge that her father had been taxed until he lost the inn he built with his own hands … it made her angry.

"What can we do?" she asked. "Honestly? The king has more men, more money, and more reach than any of us."

"That may be true now, but it won't always be that way. We've been working hard and spreading the word. More people are joining our cause every day."

"You said the rebellion is going to overthrow the king. What does that look like, exactly? Most of the people in Dawsbury aren't warriors. Are you going to march an army of farmers against the castle and demand the king step down?"

"Of course not," Tobias said. "We've been training people to fight, to defend themselves. We can't put a castle under siege. Not yet, at least. The plan is to draw Torian out of his fortress, bring him face to face with his victims. If we can cause enough problems for him out here, he'll take the bait."

It was a lot for Gwen to take in, not to mention above her head. She knew nothing of war or battle, and even less about weapons. She considered running away and leaving Dawsbury behind in the proverbial dust, but the thought of her father helping the rebellion gave her pause. If her father, an easy-going inn owner, could help people under duress, so could she.

"Where's this rebellion at? Is there a headquarters or something?"

"It's everywhere," Tobias answered. "Anywhere that people are tired of the oppression, that is where the tinder of rebellion lies. They just need a flame to ignite them."

"I—" Gwen was interrupted by shouting from the road. Tobias was peering past her, squinting. "What is it?"

"Prisoners, it looks like," Tobias replied. "They're being pulled by rope."

They waited in silence as the procession passed the cemetery. Tobias's eyes widened.

"What do you see?" Gwen asked.

"It's everyone from Boris's inn."

Gwen's heart dropped into her stomach. "Everyone?"

Tobias turned his gaze on her and Gwen was

certain he could see the fear etched on her face.

"My father, too? Is Boris with them?"

Tobias nodded.

Gwen couldn't stomach the thought of her father being held in prison. "We have to do something," she said. "We have to free him."

"We can't. There're too many soldiers. Even if you were trained with a sword, we wouldn't stand a chance."

"What about the rebellion? Won't they help one of their own?" Gwen asked.

"Of course they will, but there's a time and a place for everything we do. It'll need to be well planned. Unfortunately, we'll have to wait until they get the prisoners to the outpost. It's risky, but I think this is what we've been waiting for."

"You've been waiting for the soldiers to take prisoners?" Gwen asked, confused.

"We've been waiting for an opportunity to raze the outpost," Tobias clarified.

"Count me in," Gwen said. "I want to help rescue my father."

"I'm not in charge, but I don't think that'll be a problem with Eradore."

"Who's Air-uh-door?" Gwen asked, trying to sound out the odd name.

"He's a wizard."

CHAPTER 4

Conal

For the next three hours they lazily wended their way along the wagon trail through the thick forest. Conal responded to Lord Pharyl's questions, surprised that the Lord spent so much time with him, especially when the travel steward attempted to insert himself in the discussions.

"Beg pardon, m'Lord," the Steward interrupted. "Where would you prefer to lodge for the evening?"

Pharyl's face tightened and he raised an eyebrow. "Where do we normally spend the night?"

The man swallowed and stuttered, "I… I, um, thought that with the addition of the slaves, you might want to adjust our arrangements."

Pharyl cocked his head to the left. "What are you rambling about? How many times have I come this way with more slaves than I now have? Why are you bothering me? Is this not why I made you the travel steward, to handle these affairs?"

"Yes, Yes, m'Lord. I just wanted to make sure." He dipped his head several times. "Just making sure."

Pharyl shook his head as the man rode off to the front where the lead soldiers led the wagons on the well-traveled road.

"You see what I have to put up with?" he bemoaned. "I made him travel steward as a favor to a cousin." He turned and narrowed a stare at Conal. "Your first mission as a Cobra will be to rid me of that incompetent fool. Permanently. Understand?"

"Perfectly, m'Lord." Conal wondered what the steward had done to warrant the death sentence.

As though sensing his thoughts, Pharyl asked, "Do you not wish to know why I want him dead?"

"Is it necessary that I know, m'Lord? That you commanded it is explanation enough."

Surprised at the response, Pharyl smiled. "A wise answer. I see a great future for you. What do you know about my demesne?"

"I've traveled the breadth and width of it m'Lord. I am familiar with most towns and cities."

"And the people?"

"The same wherever I go," he gamely shrugged. "The common folk want to be left alone to go about their lives. The burgomasters run the cities and local towns, collect the taxes and skim off what's above owed to you."

"Have you been outside the demesne?" Pharyl asked, ignoring the barb at the tax burden.

"No, m'Lord, but I should like to, especially the kingdoms of the dwarves and elves. I've only ever seen them at the port towns, dwarves mostly, elves rarely."

"Sometime perhaps," Pharyl replied. "For now, it is important that you stay closer to home, learning about the demesne and its part in the kingdom. What do you know about Caldyr?"

"The king?" Conal blinked at the mention of the most powerful man in the realm.

"Yes."

"I know little, m'Lord. He is king. You rule here. That's the extent of it."

"It is time for a simple lesson," Phayrl said, assuming the role of a tutor. "There are many kingdoms in the land, some more powerful than others. Some ruled by men, others by elves and dwarves… and still others by creatures I will not talk about."

Conal pretended to pay attention, the instruction common knowledge.

"Caldyr rules the kingdom of Tir Manach, of which my realm, Vandyr, makes up a quarter if the kingdom. I rule here because Caldyr has only one son, but he has three daughters, one of whom is my wife."

Pharyl might not have been so pleased with Conal's rapt attention had he known the young man was only half listening. The other half was paying attention to the surroundings and the much too relaxed demeanor of the guards.

"Caldyr is my uncle," Pharyl droned on. "My father is, or was, his younger brother."

Conal momentarily looked away so that Pharyl would not see him rolling his eyes. While some folks lived and breathed lineage study, he'd rather watch pigs mate than listen to some dribble about an ancestor 200 years ago. He turned back and nodded, putting on his 'my-God-this-is-just-so-fascinating' face.

Noting the devoted attention, Pharyl started to explain what had happened to his father when his smile abruptly turned to a frown upon seeing the steward take the left at the fork in the road.

"No. This is wrong," he called out. "You're going the wrong way." Spurring his mount forward, he snapped, "What is wrong with that idiot."

Conal likewise spurred his horse to stay just behind Lord Pharyl whose temper increased the farther down the road he traveled. Flicking their whips to above the draft horses, the wagoners increased their speed to catch up with their disappearing Lord.

The road curved sharply to the left and Pharyl and Conal came to a sliding halt, confronted by the travel steward and Pharyl's guards surrounded by what appeared to be highwaymen. The wagons lurched to a halt, bunching up behind them.

"What's the meaning of this," Lord Pharyl demanded.

Conal did a quick assessment and calculated they were outnumbered at least two to one. The highwaymen were armed with bow and arrow, crossbows, and swords. One curious thing he noted was that they were clean and relatively well-dressed, causing him to wonder if they were who they pretended to be. Oddly enough, the steward didn't seem to be all that upset.

A tall well-built man with saucy confidence strode up and over-dramatically bowed. His auburn hair was cut short as was his beard. "Welcome my Lord. I trust your journey has been uneventful so far."

"Who are you and what do you want?"

"I am called many names," he said with a smile. "For now, 'Jock' will do… and I think you already know what we want."

Pharyl's gaze shifted from the man to his steward whose smug grin said enough. "You will pay for this with your life."

"Perhaps," the steward shrugged, "but not because of you." He nodded to an adjacent bowman who pulled back on the bowstring.

"Wait," Conal exclaimed, his hands spread. "Wait. Just hear me out. Please."

Jock ticked his head at the bowman who eased up on the bowstring.

"What are you doing?" the steward fumed at Jock before glaring at Conal. "He's a nobody, a slave." He jerked his head at Pharyl. "Kill him."

Ignoring him, Jock directed his attention to Conal. "Well?"

"I don't know what's going on, but it seems to me to be foolish to kill Lord Pharyl," Conal said, making up an excuse on the fly. "He's royalty. You kill him and you'll bring all hell down on yourselves." He held up a hand to stop Jock's interruption. "Because he's royalty… You just can't have some highwayman take out royalty anytime he wants and not expect a reaction, especially when word gets out."

"We're wasting time," the steward fussed.

Jock flipped hand at the steward telling him to be quiet. "And why would word get out?"

Conal ticked his head at the steward. "He's the one who would talk. And he'd put the entire blame on you."

"He's a liar," the steward exploded. "Why are you listening to him? We've got a job to do. Let's get on with it."

"And another thing," Conal pointed out. "Did you plan on killing all the slaves here too?"

Jock stiffened. "Of course not. You are free. I should think you would be happy about that."

"We would be, except for one little problem. If you kill Lord Pharyl, we have no letters of manumission freeing us. Therefore, we are all considered runaway slaves, and anyone can take vengeance on us."

Jock frowned then half-smiled. "Manumission. That's quite a word for a slave. I see the dressing on your shoulder, and I have to ask myself 'Why is this slave riding beside Lord Pharyl?'"

"He's marked with the Cobra," the steward interjected.

Surprised, Jock regarded Conal with new appreciation. "What is your name?"

"I am called Conal."

"You are educated?"

"Yes."

"How did you end up marked as chattel?" Jock was beginning to like this brash young man.

"Like I told our Lord here, not everyone who calls you friend is one."

"Well Conal, what do you suggest we do? We've been paid for a job and it would be bad for our reputation as highwaymen if we renege on contracts."

"You are hardly highwaymen," Conal grinned, "though I will accept the appearance for now. You've already been paid to permanently dispose of Lord Pharyl. Why? Not my business. However, like I said, killing him creates all sorts of problems for the slaves here and for the surrounding towns for you know they will bear the brunt of retribution."

Conal paused. "Instead of killing him, why not ransom him off?"

"That's crazy," the steward snapped. "You've been paid to do a job. Now do it."

"You shut up," Jock threatened then turned back to Conal. "We've already been paid. Ransoming him creates problems for us."

Conal stared intently at him. "If you were really highwaymen, it wouldn't matter."

Jock snorted a laugh. "Well spoken. I will give consideration to your suggestion."

"You can't do that," the steward exploded. "Blayne will find out what you've done."

"Blayne?" Pharyl roared. "Brody's bastard son put you up to this?" He twisted his head to focus on Jock. "Whatever he paid you, I will double it."

Jock's smile widened. "A tempting offer."

"See?" Conal said with an impish smile. "Already your prospects are improving."

Jock smirked and curled his fingers at Conal. "Come down and talk with me."

Conal dismounted and followed Jock several paces away from listening ears.

"Do you trust Pharyl to do as he said?"

"Not at all," Conal replied. "Once inside the safety of his castle, he'll state that he doesn't deal with highwaymen. But you've already been paid, so what does it matter? What matters is Blayne and his father Brody. But again, what does it matter? Now that Pharyl knows Blayne meant to kill him, he will want to return the favor. Why not offer your services to Pharyl and be paid twice for the same effort?"

Jock barked a laugh. "That is an excellent idea, with one exception. You will stay with me. I can use a man with your brains."

Conal dipped his head and smiled. "It would be a privilege." *Finally. Finally someone sees that I'm smart.*

Jock walked back to the group, Conal behind him.

"I have made my decision. Lord Pharyl and his group are free to go with the exception of Conal here."

"But he's mine," Pharyl snapped, bowing up.

Conal briskly closed the gap between him and Pharyl, motioning him to bend down. "It's all I could do, m'Lord," he whispered. "My life for yours."

Pharyl sat back up, astonished and ashamed he had this selfless man branded. "I will not forget this. I am in your debt."

"As a benefit," Jock spoke, gazing directly at Pharyl, "we will offer our services to you to eliminate the man who wished to do you harm."

Pharyl stared back at him then at Conal and immediately understood what Conal had done, impressed that this man had so easily turned the tables on his enemies. "I like your suggestion. Perhaps you can send a man to negotiate terms."

"It would be our pleasure," Jock grinned.

"What about my steward?"

"He is of no use to you," Jock answered, noting the steward's face had assumed an ashen color and he was beginning to sweat.

"I demand justice," Pharyl growled.

"A fair demand," Jock acknowledged. "Let's ask our friend here what he thinks." He turned to Conal. "What are we to do with him?" He flicked his hand at several highwaymen close by the steward who reached up and dragged him off his horse.

Conal gazed at the man held firmly between two burly men, a cockiness flowing inside him that everyone was looking to him for a solution. Everyone wanted to know what he thought should be done. *This is a nice change from Oscon.*

"You know he can't be trusted," Conal sagely stated. "He was more than willing to betray his Lord for who knows how much. Ask him. How much was it?"

Jock shifted a glance at the steward. "Well? Answer the man."

When he didn't answer, one of the men holding him poked him in the side with a dagger.

"Fifty regals," he sputtered with a hard swallow.

"Fifty regals," Conal repeated in a loud voice. "The man betrayed a Lord for a mere fifty regals. I assume they were gold regals. Apparently a Lord's life isn't worth much… unless they promised him something more." He folded his arms and stared at the steward.

Realizing his life was on tender hooks, the steward blurted, "And a pub of my own."

"There you have it," Conal announced as though he were a barrister playing to a jury. "The man sold out for a mere fifty regals and a pint of ale. What makes you think he won't betray you when the time is right… and for a lot less than fifty regals?"

"You're right," Jock agreed with a nod.

"Wait," the steward struggled. "You can't do this. We had a deal. Blayne will make you pay for this. Please."

With an extravagant display, Jock slowly looked around the group. "What say you? Death or life?"

The shouts of 'Death' reverberated. Jock turned to look up at Pharyl whose pleased demeanor told him his answer. Yet Pharyl nodded and added his own voice to the crescendo.

"O God, please no," the steward begged, sinking to his knees.

Jock walked over to one of his highwaymen. Taking the man's crossbow, he strode back to Conal and thrust it into his hands.

"Here. Kill him."

CHAPTER 5

Gwen

An hour after departing the cemetery outside Dawsbury, Gwen and Tobias were nearing the outpost that the prisoners had been escorted to. Gwen had spent much of the walk deep in thought. Tobias had thrown so much information at her, and she was still working through it all. When she spotted the outpost, she stopped walking.

"I thought we were going to see Eradore?"

"We are," Tobias replied. "His place is past the outpost."

"Aren't you afraid the soldiers will see you?"

"Not really. I don't think the men we encountered will remember my face from the many others they've seen today. Besides, it was dark. If any of them happened to memorize what they saw, I'd be impressed."

Gwen wrung her hands anxiously, but she reminded herself that she agreed to trust Tobias and this would be the first opportunity to prove her word. She nodded at him and continued walking.

"Besides, we're going to need a horse, maybe two. How much do you weigh?"

"That's none of your business," Gwen snapped. "And I didn't know the soldiers sold horses at the outpost."

"They don't," Tobias said. "We're going to steal one."

"I'm sorry? I don't think I heard you correctly.

You said we're going to steal a horse from the king's soldiers?"

"It sounds to me like you've got great hearing."

Gwen shot a glare at Tobias, but he was grinning from ear to ear. "You must think yourself amusing," she said.

"Absolutely. Life is too short for delusions." Tobias chuckled at his own joke, but Gwen rolled her eyes.

"Don't worry. I've done this several times. We'll be long gone before they even know a horse is missing. Trust me."

There were far too many warning signs for Gwen's comfort, but she was determined to keep her word. Tobias was proving to be brash and overconfident, but he was the only person Gwen had right now.

Tobias took them off the road, keeping a wide berth of the outpost until they passed it, then circled back and hid among the shadows of a copse of trees. Gwen was tempted to ask why he wasted the effort, but then she spotted the stable. It was a squat wood building with a thatched roof outside of the main compound. A lantern hung next to each of the stalls, illuminating the area more than Gwen was comfortable with.

"Stay here and wait for me. Once I'm free of the stable, you need to be prepared for a hasty exit. We're going to fly like the wind."

"What about all that light? Someone is bound to see you moving around."

"The lanterns are new, but that just makes my job easier," Tobias said. "I don't have to fumble around in the dark."

"What if something goes wrong? What should I do?" Gwen looked around for anything that might be used as a weapon, but aside from a few busted wagon wheels, she didn't spot anything useful.

"If I whistle, that means go."

"Go … where?" Gwen asked.

"Anywhere, just get away from here. Find somewhere to lie low and wait a day or two, then head to Penshaw and find an elf named Muriel. She'll get you to Eradore."

"Just get a horse and get back here," Gwen said.

"Yes, my lady." Tobias offered a mock bow and sprinted to the stable.

Gwen watched fretfully until Tobias entered one of the stalls. She looked around to make sure there were no soldiers, but the trees blocked part of her view. She crept closer to the edge of the tree line and stopped when she smelled urine. The scent was strong and burned her nostrils. A few more steps revealed the source of the smell.

A makeshift latrine had been dug in front of the trees. Gwen pinched her nose shut and finished surveying the area. It was quiet and she didn't see a single soldier, which she found odd. *Shouldn't someone be on watch or something?* she wondered.

The door to the stall Tobias had entered opened, its hinges creaking. Gwen flinched, expecting the entire garrison to come pouring out of the outpost. Instead, Tobias led a dappled mare out and then mounted it. He flicked the reins and the horse took off with a burst of speed. Gwen turned and ran through the trees, breaking free of the copse and ending up on the road.

She saw Tobias approaching quickly, but she noticed another horse following him. A black-clad soldier rode on its back and lifted something up. A moment later, there was a whizzing sound and Tobias let out a cry of anguish. He remained on the horse, and as he neared Gwen, he leaned over the side and stretched out his arm.

Gwen jogged toward him and grabbed ahold of his hand, using her momentum and his strength to shoot upward and land on the saddle behind him. She wrapped her arms around him and felt something wet and warm against her arm. Tobias flicked the reins again and rammed his heels into the horse's flanks, urging the beast to go faster. Gwen looked back and saw the mounted soldier wasn't following them.

Roughly a mile down the road revealed why as Tobias grunted and slouched forward, almost falling off the horse. Gwen jerked the reins from him and slowed their pace, giving the horse a reprieve but also allowing her to look over Tobias. She found a crossbow bolt lodged in his side and an alarming amount of blood soaked into his shirt.

"Tobias, can you hear me?"

The man was unconscious. Gwen considered removing the bolt, but she didn't know if that would help or further injure him, so she left it alone. She had seen the results of barroom brawls before, but this was something entirely different. He needed a healer, and they weren't anywhere near one.

Gwen managed to pull Tobias into her lap and got the horse to move faster, but nowhere near the breakneck pace Tobias had. She assumed they would have to ride through the night before they reached the nearest town, but when she spotted a farmhouse a while later, she whispered a heartfelt thanks to the sky and stopped the horse. Gwen laid Tobias on the horse's neck and slid off the saddle, then ran to the front door of the house and knocked loudly. The door opened and an older man peered out at her.

"My friend needs help! He's lost a lot of blood and needs a healer."

The man looked from her to the horse. "Me and Gail ain't healers, but she can stitch him up. Help me bring him inside." He stepped out of the house and shouted over his shoulder, "Gail! Get out here, woman!"

Gwen helped the man pull Tobias from the saddle, and they awkwardly carried him into the house. The man guided Gwen into the kitchen, and they laid Tobias on the table. It creaked under Tobias's weight, but it held firmly.

"What happened?" Gail asked, her voice low and frail.

"I'd say he was hit by a crossbow," the man said, pointing to the bolt in Tobias's side.

"Let me get my things. Errol, be a dear and get me a bowl of water and some cloth."

The two left the kitchen. Gwen looked at Tobias's still form. The bolt had pierced his right side, just above the hip. His cobalt-hued shirt was dark with blood, and more seeped from the wound, dripping onto the table. Gail returned first, holding a needle and thread.

"Have you ever tended a wound?" she asked.

"Never," Gwen answered.

"Some don't have the stomach for it, but when you've lived with animals long enough, you get used to some ugly sights."

Errol carried a wooden bowl half-filled with water and a bolt of cloth under his arm. He pulled a chair out from the table and set the bowl on it, then started unrolling the cloth, cutting it into strips.

"I'm not one to pry," Errol said as he worked, "but what brings you two out to the country at this hour?"

"We were on our way to see … a friend," Gwen said. "Before we were attacked."

Errol frowned. "The road used to be safe from brigands. Lately, though …" He exchanged looks with Gail. "Well, lately there've been problems."

"The soldiers?" Gwen boldly asked.

"Yes," Gail said. "They come through our land sometimes, picking from our crops and stealing our chickens."

Gail gently pulled Tobias's shirt away from the wound, then examined the bolt. "Errol—"

"Yeah, yeah," Errol muttered. "'Be a dear and pull the bolt out.' I got it, woman."

Gwen averted her gaze, unsure she could stomach the gruesome sight.

"There we go," Errol said, and Gwen looked back at Tobias and immediately regretted it. More blood flowed from the wound. Gail cupped her hands and dipped them into the bowl, then poured the water onto Tobias's damaged flesh. Tobias groaned and his head lolled to the side, but he remained unconscious.

Gwen felt faint. All the blood was making her queasy. Errol took notice and motioned for her to follow him.

"Holler if you need anything," he told Gail. She waved him off, focused on her work. He led Gwen out of the house and around to the back.

"He's not fit for travel, so you're going to need somewhere to stay for the night. We don't have room in the house, but you can stay in the barn. The nights have been warm, so you shouldn't need a fire, but if you do, keep it away from the walls."

"Thank you for the offer, but I don't think we should stay here," Gwen said.

"I know the lodging I'm offering isn't the best, but it's all we have."

"It's not that. I just don't think it's wise to stay in one place too long right now." Gwen looked in the direction they'd traveled from. The road was empty, but something was telling her to keep moving.

Errol nodded wordlessly. "I understand. You're free to risk it, but I think your friend is going to need the rest. Jouncing around on a horse will likely break the sutures Gail's stitching."

Gwen was torn. She knew Tobias needed to rest, but she was certain the soldiers were going to come looking for them. "I guess a few hours won't hurt," she said. "I don't have any money to give you. I suppose I should have mentioned that earlier."

"There's no charge for kindness," Errol said. "Don't worry about payment. Just take care of your friend."

"Thank you."

After Gail had stitched Tobias's wound closed, the three of them carried him to the barn and laid him on a makeshift bed of straw. Gail covered him with a clean blanket, and Errol brought the stolen horse in, tying its reins to a post.

"If you decide to stay for the night, you should take the saddle off him," Errol said.

Gwen nodded and sat beside Tobias.

"He should be fine, so long as he doesn't tear the stitches," Gail said. "I know you want to be on your way, but I suggest letting him rest until morning."

"I'll keep that in mind," Gwen replied.

The couple left her a lantern and returned to the house. Gwen watched the light cast flickering shadows along the walls. She was suddenly overcome with exhaustion. Her muscles ached and her eyes were growing heavy. She stood up and paced around the barn, trying to stay awake.

Eventually, she grew tired of being on her feet and used some hay as a chair. She stared at Tobias and pondered the things he'd told her. If he wasn't lying, who were her real parents? Had they given her up because they didn't want her, or because they couldn't give her the life they wanted her to have?

Gwen's eyes shot open, and she realized she had dozed off. She stood up and looked around, trying to determine what woke her. Tobias was in the same position, his eyes still closed. A sound outside caught her attention, and she peeked out of the barn.

A group of mounted soldiers were outside the farmhouse. One of them was on foot, standing at the front door. Gwen saw Errol was talking with him. He pointed to the road, waving his hand westward.

Gwen held her breath, hoping the soldiers would leave. The one on foot shouted something and struck Errol in the face, knocking the man to the ground. Gwen covered her mouth in horror, stifling a scream. She looked at the horse, then at Tobias. There was no way she could lift him onto the saddle herself. That left only one option. She would have to—

"Where am I?"

It was Tobias. Gwen rushed to his side. She put a finger to her lips and shook her head, then mouthed the word 'soldiers.' Tobias's face scrunched in confusion. Gwen leaned down and whispered in his ear.

"The soldiers are here."

Tobias closed his eyes. "We need to go," he rasped.

"I'm with you on that, but you're injured."

"Better injured than dead. Help me up."

Gwen grabbed Tobias's hands and pulled with everything she had. A pained expression covered Tobias's face, but he only grunted softly. Gwen was impressed. She would have screamed in agony. Tobias hovered a hand over the bandage Gail had wrapped over the wound.

"Is this your handiwork?" he asked.

"Hardly," Gwen answered. "If I help you, can you get on the horse?"

"I think so."

Gwen retrieved the lantern and hung it on the wall near the horse, then struggled to assist Tobias into the saddle. A long moment of frustration gave way to victory and Tobias was seated. The lantern illuminated his face and Gwen saw a haggard and pale complexion. Tobias grabbed the reins and turned the horse toward the barn doors.

"Take my hand," he said.

"I can manage," Gwen replied. She struck her foot in the stirrup and flung herself upward. The first two times she didn't get high enough to get her leg over the horse, but the third time she succeeded.

The horse clopped over to the doors just as they swung open. Three soldiers were there on foot, swords drawn. Gwen's breath caught in her throat, but Tobias kicked the horse and yelled, "Yah!"

The soldiers scrambled out of the way as the mare burst forth from the barn. Shouts rose, and Gwen saw the mounted soldiers were pursuing them.

"They're coming!" she shouted.

"We can lose them in the woods," Tobias cried back.

Gwen couldn't make out much detail of the landscape, but she did see tall shadows that rose from the ground and guessed they were trees. Tobias spurred the horse, and it sped across the farmland, the air whipping Gwen's hair about wildly. She kept looking back, hoping the soldiers would give up their chase, but there was no such luck. They were still there, but they hadn't gotten any closer.

They reached the woods and Tobias turned the horse to the right, guiding it to a brook. The water moved slowly and wasn't very high.

"This should throw them off," Tobias said, forcing the horse into the water. They headed upstream, traveling for a long while in silence. They left the woods behind and were greeted by rolling green hills. Once the water started to get deeper, Tobias took them back onto dry land and stopped atop one of the hills to stare back the way they'd come.

"I think we lost them," he said, his voice little more than a whisper.

Gwen wasn't certain, but she thought she saw movement down by the stream. "What's that?" she asked, pointing.

Tobias stared for a moment, then his eyes widened. "Impossible," he choked. "They're still tracking us."

CHAPTER 6

Conal

Conal stared at the crossbow in his hands, the bolt notched and ready. Silence had smothered the forest as those surrounding him waited. He looked up to see the steward five paces away, cringing in abject terror, the two highwaymen gripping him by the arms, holding him up. His brilliant design of extricating himself had gone painfully wrong and he wondered if they knew he had never killed a man before. Not that he hadn't wanted to on more than a few occasions, but wanting and actually doing were two vastly different affairs.

"Well, come on," Jock urged. "We don't have all day."

With a grin of false bravado, Conal shifted his gaze to him. "Hardly seems sporting. How can I miss?"

"That's the point," Jock answered. "You're not supposed to miss."

"I know, but where's the fun of killing an unarmed man held firmly in one spot?"

"You want to give him a chance?" Jock raised an eyebrow.

"Why not?" An idea blossomed along with his confidence. "Give him a five second head start down the road. Make it interesting."

Jock sniffed a laugh. "Alright." Turning to the steward, he pointed down the road. "You've got five seconds. If he misses, you live." He looked back at Conal. "You ready?"

"Ready and waiting," Conal cheerfully replied, shifting position on the road and raising the crossbow to his shoulder.

With their attention focused on Conal and the steward, they didn't notice Pharyl's stern wave at another highwayman, demanding the man's crossbow. Despite initial misgiving and after repeated silent demands, the man handed the weapon to him.

"You can let go of him," Jock commanded the two men holding the steward. Staring directly at the steward, he pointed to the road behind the terrified man. "Let's see how fast you can run. Go."

The steward spun around and gave panic to his legs, churning as fast as he could, hearing Jock announce, "One… two… three… four…" pause, "five."

Conal took aim at the disappearing steward. Despite having never killed a man, he was more than proficient with a crossbow, this time aiming just to the left of the man's head.

In the interval between Conal's aim and squeezing the trigger-lever, Pharyl stood in the stirrups, aimed and launched his bolt, hitting the steward squarely between the shoulder blades, causing him to stumble enough to the left that Conal's bolt rammed into the back of the man's head.

"Ouch," Jock smirked. "That's gonna leave a bruise." Turning back to Conal, he complimented, "Nice shot," adding, "and you too," to Lord Pharyl. "I will send a man to you to negotiate our bargain to eliminate Blayne."

Conal's mouth had dropped open the moment his bolt whipped the man's head forward. Now rooted to the ground, he fumbled with his emotions. In truth, the steward meant nothing to him. Had Conal continued in Pharyl's employ as a Cobra he would have had the man killed per Pharyl's instructions, but someone else would have done the killing. His hands would be clean. But was there a difference… really? Still, the steward was a traitor and needed to be dealt with. Besides, it was Lord Pharyl's bolt that killed the man.

Conal's introspection was interrupted when Jock circled his finger in the air and called out to his band, "Let's get ready to move out."

Conal hustled several steps to catch up with him. "What about the slaves?"

"What about them?"

"Manumission?"

Jock shook his head. "Not my problem, not my call."

Though disappointed, Conal understood. Now was not the time to press the issue. Looking back over his shoulder, he saw Pharyl waiting to speak with him.

"I am sorely disappointed I am losing your services," Pharyl gravely said.

"Who knows where the future lies, m'Lord. I still proudly wear your mark." He dipped his head towards the bandaged shoulder.

Pharyl sat back in his saddle, peering intently at the young man before loudly declaring, "To all who stand here now as witness, I declare Conal to be a free man." He narrowed his gaze at Jock. "When you send your man to see me, I will give him the necessary papers."

"Thank you, m'Lord." Conal bowed and inwardly grinned. He had yet again got himself out of a mess.

Gathering the reins, Pharyl nodded and resumed his march, two of his guards having already moved the steward off the road into the forest where carrion fowl and animals would feast upon the body.

Waiting until Pharyl was down the road, Jock wryly commented, "While he gave you your freedom, I notice he took your horse."

"It was his to begin with," Conal shrugged with a smile. "So. What's the plan?"

"We head on home. Walk with me." Jock led the way into the forest, Conal dodging trees and bushes to keep up. "Tell me about yourself. Where are you from?"

"Urve."

"On the coast?"

"Yes."

Jock tossed a quizzical glance at him. "How did you end up in Hamlyn?"

"My father decided I needed to be educated, so he sent me to the priory in Ecclesley. Not liking their method of education, I escaped when I was fifteen, knocked around for a couple of years refining my inept skill of thievery then threw in my lot with a man called Oscon."

"I've heard of him."

Conal scowled. "I hope to meet him again in

better circumstances when I can plunge a knife in his throat. It is because of him that I wear this brand."

Jock glanced at him then quickly surveyed the men and women scattered around him. "How is it that you were branded a Cobra?"

"I'd love to say because of my formidable abilities, but honestly, I haven't a clue."

Jock chuckled. "You think fast on your feet, which is a good thing. We'll need that where we're going."

"I thought we were going to help Pharyl," Conal said.

"We are… but not yet. I'll explain later."

Accepting the response for the moment, Conal asked, "Who are you… when you're not Jock?"

Jock grinned, impressed once again with the young man. "I am Rhonyn."

Conal held on to his next question when he saw them, the horses, a man and a woman guarding them.

"You can either ride double or walk," Rhonyn said. "Your choice."

A man emerged from a thicket and languidly walked towards Rhonyn. He was tall, with a full dark-brown beard, thick hair that fell below his shoulders, and coal black eyes. He dressed like a huntsman with tight dark green leggings in calf-high leather boots, and a brown leather vest over a forest green long-sleeved shirt. A supple leather bag of lamb skin held by a shoulder strap bounced on his left hip as he walked. His right hand held a staff of polished oak topped with a dragon's head. As the man walked up, Conal couldn't tell if he was looking at Rhonyn or him for the eyes were solid and opaque. The man stopped and swiveled his head to gaze at Conal, at least that's what it felt like.

"This him?" The man's voice was an odd contrast to his dress for the voice had a resonant hum of tranquility, the softness of peace.

"Yes," Rhonyn answered.

"Where you from lad?"

"Urve," Conal replied, a bit unnerved by the sightless eyes. "Who are you?"

"This is Drustan," Rhonyn answered for him, "the half-druid."

"Which half?" Conal said without thinking, causing Rhonyn to giggle and Drustan to stiffen.

"He means no harm," Rhonyn soothed then turned to Conal. "You would do well to curb your quick tongue on occasion. Do you not know what a half-druid is?"

"Uh… no." Conal had heard of druids, but half-druids?

"A half-druid," Rhonyn explained, "is a druid bonded with an undead soul."

"Sounds painful," Conal quipped.

"Have a care, lad," the druid snapped, straining to maintain his soothing voice. "Do not mock that which you don't know or understand. Hold out your hand."

"Why?" Conal usually didn't dislike someone from the start, but this guy was an exception.

"Do it," Drustan commanded.

"I say again," Conal stubbornly replied, "why?"

"Because I told you so." The half-druid's voice

morphed to a brittle harshness.

"Just do it, please," Rhonyn said, carefully watching the interaction.

Figuring they weren't going to let it go until he obeyed, Conal reluctantly stuck out his hand.

The half-druid grasped Conal's hand and closed his eyes.

Conal felt a searing pain shoot throughout his body and he yelped as he worked to pry his hand free, but the druid's strength was far too strong. It was like Conal had gotten his hand stuck in a rock crevasse and despite his wild flailing, the rock never moved. The pain increased along with an intense heat until he felt he was going to explode and melt at the same time.

The druid let go and Conal careened backwards, tumbling onto the ground.

"What the hell," Conal yelled, clutching his hand.

"Well?" Rhonyn said, looking at Drustan.

"I could not see the birth-mind," the half-druid answered, looking at Conal who shook his hand, trying to cool it off. "His other memories are of Urve and a sense of despair at the separation from his father." He bent forward slightly to focus on Conal. "Are you telling me the truth?"

"I haven't said anything," Conal snarled. "You nearly killed me."

"I know," he nodded. "That's what bothers me." He brusquely turned to Rhonyn. "He has strength far beyond a mere wharf-rat."

"I'm not a wharf-rat," Conal growled. "My father is a jewelry merchant and a very successful one. So get your story straight."

Drustan tilted his head to look at the bulge beneath the shirt on Conal's shoulder. "You wear a brand. Shall we look at it?"

"Why?"

Drustan chuckled. "To see how it heals."

Though curious himself, Conal didn't like the thought that this half-wit… uh, half-druid wanted to see it.

"Tell me," the druid said. "Does it still hurt?"

Conal frowned in thought, realizing that the pain had stopped as soon as the branding iron lifted from his arm. "No, not really."

Drustan nodded. "Come. Let us see how well it heals."

Conal hesitated then unbuttoned his shirt and reached up and unwrapped the thin cloth surrounding the brand.

Drustan reached out to touch it and jerked his hand back as though stung. "A Cobra head." He stepped back, shaking his head. "This all wrong. It doesn't fit."

"Doesn't fit what?" Conal demanded before glancing down at the brand, not surprised that his scar had completely healed and the brand itself looked quite good.

Instead of answering, the half-druid spun around and stalked off.

"What's with him?" Conal sniffed.

Rhonyn bent down to study Conal's brand, looked up at Conal then swiveled his head to watch the half-druid flop down beneath an oak tree. "Your scar has healed."

"So it seems." Conal nonchalantly replied.

"You were branded this morning?"

"Yes."

Rhonyn stood back up. "Do you not find this unusual?"

"I was always a fast healer," he shrugged.

Rhonyn shook his head. "Not this fast."

"You mind telling me what's going on?"

Rhonyn stared at him a moment before saying, "We are searching for someone."

"Who?"

"A king's son."

"What does that have to do with me?" He put his shirt back on.

"You are the right age."

Conal paused to button his shirt and barked a disbelieving laugh. "Me? Are you daft? My father's a jeweler. I've been a highwayman for these past several years. I've just been branded as an outlaw. What's wrong with you people? You round up guys my age and let Grip and Grin over there roast them to see if they might be a king. What's wrong with this picture?"

"I know it sounds strange," Rhonyn grinned, "but there are reasons behind it."

"So who is this king anyway?"

"His name was Kamron."

"Was? So sometime along the way, this guy loses his kid then dies and now you're trying to find the kid?"

"Kids. There's a girl too."

Conal shook his head in disgust. "This is the stuff of fairy tales. Next you're gonna tell me that you guys work for some evil king who wants to kill the kids because they're the rightful heirs to the throne."

When Rhonyn remained silent, Conal threw up his hands. "I was making a joke. Please tell me you're not serious."

"We are," Rhonyn quietly replied, "and you can help us."

"How? I don't know any royalty, let alone any king's kids. And why would I want to throw in my lot with an evil king? By definition he's bad. You actually think something good is going to come of this?"

"There's far more going on than I can explain or that you would understand," Rhonyn said. "Besides, you got something better to do?"

"Yeah. I could go learn to be a Cobra."

"Maybe later," Rhonyn firmly said. "For now, you're one of us."

"Just great," Conal fumed and stomped off to mingle with the horses who were probably the only sane creatures around here.

Rhonyn watched him trudge away before turning to walk over where Drustan sat. "What did you see?"

"He is a conundrum. He has the aura of the one we search for, but he has too many inconsistencies. His birth-mind is blank before nursing. That alone gives me cause to suspect. And his healing. Another factor. And he endured the limits of my strength. However, he bears the Cobra Head."

"So?"

Drustan lifted his eyes to stare at Rhonyn. "The

eagle will bear the vipers in its claws, yet from the west a cobra will rise and strike down the eagle."

Rhonyn shook his head. "That means nothing to me."

Drustan curled a lip. "The eagle is King Torian. The vipers are Kamron's children. The cobra is the unknown assassin who will claim the throne as his own."

Rhonyn looked back over his shoulder at Conal who was nuzzling one of the horses. "What do you want to do?"

"We can take no chances. We must kill him."

CHAPTER 7

Gwen

"How are they still following us?" Gwen asked, shouting to be heard above the mare's thunderous galloping.

If Tobias replied, Gwen didn't hear him. She held onto him tightly as they covered more ground and was careful not to touch near his wound. They rode until the hills flattened into grassland, and Gwen constantly looked back to watch their pursuers.

The sun was beginning to crest over the horizon and Gwen spotted a walled city up the road. She'd never been this far from home and was officially lost. Without Tobias, she probably wouldn't have made it this far.

"She doesn't have much left in her," Tobias said, patting the mare's neck comfortingly. "Good thing we're almost there."

"Is that where Eradore is?" Gwen asked.

"Yes. So long as we can reach the gates before the soldiers catch up to us, we can lose them for good in the city."

"Are you sure? Your little water trick didn't help."

Tobias was silent for a moment, then said, "I think they're using magic. That's the only explanation for how they've kept on our trail."

"Magic?" The world suddenly seemed much larger than Gwen had ever imagined. Plots to overthrow a king, soldiers chasing commoners across the countryside, and magic. It was too much at once.

"Do you always repeat what people say, or do you just do it to annoy me?" Tobias asked.

Gwen bumped him with her shoulder and then realized her mistake when Tobias hissed in a breath. "Sorry," she said. "I forgot."

"Don't worry about it. I'll get used to the pain. Besides, I've had worse injuries than this. I just need a few days to rest and I'll be back to myself again."

"So what happens when we meet with Eradore? Will you tell him what happened at the inn and then organize the rebellion to attack the outpost?"

"Something like that," Tobias said evasively.

"Can you get the horse to move any faster?"

"Only if you want to kill her," Tobias replied.

"If it's between her life and ours, I say do whatever you need to. The soldiers are getting closer."

Tobias twisted in the saddle, his face scrunching in pain, and looked behind them. "Blast it," he grunted. "I'm sorry, girl," he told the horse, then snapped the reins. The mare picked up the pace, but not by much.

As they drew closer to the city of Penshaw, there were more signs of life. Cottages and livestock dotted the landscape, and they passed a few slow-moving wagons filled with vegetables. Gwen's stomach growled as if telling her it was time to eat. *Safety before food,* she told herself.

The city gates were wide open, allowing anyone free access in or out. The horse slowed down to a tired trot, and they passed through the wall without issue. Gwen looked up at the raised portcullis and pictured a morbid image of it closing down on them. She chalked it up to her lack of sleep and turned her attention to the vast array of vendors, stalls, and people that filled the streets.

Gwen smelled so many wonderful scents drifting on the air, and they all made her mouth water. Tobias guided the horse down a street to the left and stopped outside a building with several horses tethered to wooden poles.

"We need to get rid of the horse and find somewhere to hide before the soldiers find us," Tobias said. "I'm going to need your help dismounting."

Gwen slid off the side of the mare and offered her hands to Tobias. He accepted one and tried to ease himself down, but ended up slipping out of the saddle and landing on the ground with enough force to cause his bandage to stain with fresh blood. He grimaced and bit his lower lip.

"Wait here with the horse," he grunted.

"Where are you going?" Gwen asked, glancing

around uneasily.

"Inside to sell the horse. Weren't you listening?"

Gwen rolled her eyes at Tobias as he went inside the building. She turned to watch the gates and fidgeted with the horse's reins. The Seven Stars was one of the largest buildings in Dawsbury, but it paled in comparison to ones around her now. Everything was big, from the buildings to the wall that stretched around the city.

Tobias returned and tossed a small bag to her. She caught it, the coins inside clinking together.

"Is this for me?" she asked.

Tobias laughed, then grimaced and clenched his fists. He took a breath. "No, it's *ours*. I just want you to hold onto it."

Gwen shrugged and hid the bag in the waistband of her pants. "Where to now?"

"We need somewhere to hide until we can get word to Eradore that we need a meeting. There's an inn nearby we can rent a room from."

"What about the soldiers?" Gwen asked.

"They're going to have a rough time searching for us. Penshaw is the city that never rests, so people are always coming and going. Once we're holed up in the inn, their search will be almost impossible."

"What if they're using magic?"

"That's why I said *almost*. Eradore will know if

they are using magic. He's some sort of rare type of wizard or something. Anyway, let's get moving."

Tobias led Gwen along the backstreets where there were few people. He explained to her that it would have been easier to take the road at the gates straight down the middle of the city, but they were more likely to be spotted.

After a half hour of walking along cobbled stone streets, they reached an inn with a wooden sign that read *The Burrow*. It was tall like the buildings around it and music could be heard playing inside. Gwen felt a pang of sadness, thinking about the bard from the Seven Stars. Had he been imprisoned too?

The interior of the inn was radically different than the Seven Stars. A massive hearth sat in the center of the room, the façade crafted of white square stones stacked atop each other and lined with lime mortar. The floors were birch wood, which reflected the light that poured in from the many windows.

Tobias headed for the bar and Gwen followed, pausing briefly to look around at the host of people who were enjoying breakfast and the music. The people were lively given the hour, and Gwen spotted plates full of steaming eggs, fresh bread, and sausage.

"Gwen!"

She looked at Tobias. He was motioning for her to come to the bar.

"Stop gawking and get over here."

She joined him, and he held his hand out. "The money, please," he said. Gwen pulled the bag out and handed it to him, then continued looking around the inn. The place was packed with all different races. Gwen saw mostly elves, dwarves, and humans, but there was also a single gnome sitting by himself.

"We just need one room," she heard Tobias say.

"One?" Gwen asked, turning to the barkeep. At first glance, she thought the stocky dwarf behind the counter was a male, but then the dwarf spoke and the voice was feminine.

"I'll sleep on the floor if it makes you feel better," Tobias said.

"We've only got one room available anyway," the barkeep replied.

"We'll take it," Tobias confirmed.

"How many nights will you be staying?"

"I'm not sure yet. Two, maybe three." Tobias opened the bag and poured half of the coins onto the counter. "Will that cover the room and some food?" Tobias pulled his sleeve up and flashed his wrist at the dwarf. It was subtle and Gwen almost missed the move. She looked at Tobias questioningly but he ignored her.

"That's plenty," the barkeep answered. She set a key on the counter. "Third floor, last room on the left."

"Much appreciated," Tobias said. He passed the key to Gwen and they took a seat at the only empty table available, which was next to the gnome. Gwen stared at the curious creature from her periphery until she saw Tobias frowning at her.

"What are you doing?" he asked.

"Nothing."

"Didn't Boris teach you that staring is rude?"

"Sorry. I'm curious is all." Gwen rubbed her eyes and stifled a yawn.

The barkeep delivered two plates of food to their table along with two tankards of ale. Gwen wasted little time in eating. She devoured everything on the plate and offered a contented sigh.

"That was good, but it's too early for ale," she said.

"I'll drink yours, then," Tobias said. The color had returned to his face, and he didn't look like he was on the brink of death anymore.

"How do we get word to Eradore?" Gwen asked.

"Keep your voice down," Tobias admonished. "You never know who might be listening." He took a long drink from his tankard, then leaned forward over the table. "There's a network of people here in Penshaw who move messages for the rebellion. We'll leave a message for one, and when Eradore gets it, he'll find us."

"Where do you find these secret messengers?" Gwen asked.

Tobias smiled. "You're eager, aren't you?"

"I want my father rescued," Gwen replied. "Once he's safe, I'll feel better."

"I know. One step at a time." Tobias turned around to look at the gnome and offered a slight nod. The gnome rose from his chair and came over to their table. He stood a little over three feet in height and wore spectacles that kept sliding down his enlarged nose. His head was bald but he sported a long white beard.

"The swan flies low and the alligator draws near," Tobias said.

Gwen's brows creased in confusion. The gnome scratched his bulbous nose and pushed his spectacles up high, which made his eyes appear to grow in size. He shuffled on his way and disappeared through the inn's door.

"Did he understand what you said? —because I didn't."

"It's a coded phrase," Tobias replied. "In the event a messenger is interrogated by our enemy, the message won't make any sense."

"That's clever," Gwen said. "I would never have thought of something like that. So, do we wait here for him to return?"

"No. The return message will be delivered by someone else. We can go upstairs and get some rest while we wait."

"How will the new messenger know where to find us?"

Tobias inched his sleeve up to reveal a small tattoo of a swan. "Everyone part of the rebellion takes the mark. It's how we identify our allies. The room we've been given is specifically for people like us."

"Wait. I saw you flash your wrist to the dwarf. The barkeep is part of the rebellion?"

"Valmutrude isn't technically part of the rebellion. She plays a part much like Boris, allowing us to funnel information and other things through the inn. In some ways, she takes more risk than we do."

Gwen watched Valmutrude bustle about the inn and viewed her with a newfound respect.

"Come on," Tobias rose from the table. "I'm sure you could use some sleep."

Gwen got up and followed Tobias up the stairs located in the back-left corner of the inn. They reached the door Valmutrude had specified, and Gwen unlocked it and pushed it open. The bed called her name, and she rushed inside and threw herself on it.

"If you need anything from me, you might want to tell me now. Once I close my eyes, I'm out."

Tobias chuckled. "I'm fine. Get some rest. I'll wake you when we get word from Eradore."

Gwen closed her eyes. The next thing she knew, Tobias was gently shaking her shoulder. Hadn't she just fallen asleep? She blinked a few times, fighting off the sleep that tried to reclaim her.

"What is it?" she asked.

"Eradore wants to see us."

"Is he here?" Gwen sat up and wiped the sleep from her eyes. Her muscles no longer ached, but she was still exhausted.

"No. He said he can't leave his tower, so we must go to him."

"Oh." Gwen stretched languidly and climbed out of the bed. "How do we get there? Is a carriage coming to get us or something?"

"Or something," Tobias replied. He held out his hand to reveal a clear stone.

"What's that?"

"It's a key."

"That's an odd key," Gwen said, the skepticism evident in her tone.

"It's a magical key," Tobias clarified. "I don't suppose you've ever traveled through a magical gateway before?"

Something about his words jarred Gwen's mind, and she started to recall a distant memory, but then it was gone.

"Are you all right?" Tobias asked.

"What? Yes, yes, I'm fine. I think I'm still a

little tired."

"If you say so," Tobias replied. "Anyway, have you?"

"No," Gwen said. "I've never seen magic before, unless you count the old man who came to Seven Stars that did card tricks."

"That's not real magic," Tobias chided. "You're going to love this."

A slender mirror hung on the wall, roughly four feet long and two feet wide. Tobias walked over to it and pressed the stone to the glass, then traced a symbol over its surface. There was a scratching noise as he slid the stone around, but the mirror remained untouched. When he finished, the glass surface rippled like liquid.

"After you," Tobias said, motioning to the portal.

"You can go," Gwen said, feeling nervous.

"Ladies first," Tobias insisted.

Gwen gave him an unamused stare, then stepped up to the mirror and hesitated. It looked like a normal mirror aside from the constant rippling. Gwen took a deep breath, then touched the glass. Her hand slowly disappeared and she quickly pulled back.

"I don't know if I can do this."

"You'll be fine," Tobias said. "Trust me."

Gwen wanted to ask him what his obsession with trust was, but instead she kept her mouth shut.

She thought about her father imprisoned, and that bolstered her courage enough to force her to step into the portal. Tobias's words echoed in her mind briefly, and then …

… the world erupted in fire and pain.

CHAPTER 8

Conal

Pretending to scratch the horse's cheek, Conal peered over the muzzle to watch Rhonyn and the half-druid, noting their not so surreptitious glances in his direction. He particularly didn't like the cold look on Drustan's face, the experience of the intense pain bursting from the man's simple handshake still fresh. The rest of Rhonyn's group spread out and patiently waited, lounging against trees and chatting quietly amongst themselves.

Instinct told him he needed to scoot while he still had a chance. A quick glance at the others showed that those with crossbows had released the bow string and removed the bolt, slipping it into the leather holders with the rest of their bolts.

"You like my horse," a woman said, walking up. She was half a head shorter than Conal, with dirty blond hair and a pert nose. Though dressed as a supposed highwayman in dark leggings and tunic, she had the aura of one in costume. A quiver filled with arrows dangled at her left hip, an unstrung bow in her right hand.

"Yes. I've always loved horses." He smiled at her but his focus slipped past her face to where Rhonyn nodded at something the druid had said and shot a quick glance at Conal before calling an archer over. It was the way Rhonyn turned his shoulder so that Conal could not see the hand gestures.

Call it intuition or whatever, but warning alarms erupted inside him along with the overwhelming need to flee.

"Uh… if you'll excuse me, I need to find a place to… uh…" He smiled self-consciously.

The woman grinned in understanding and pointed to a thick copse about ten paces beyond where they stood. "That's the men's spot, just on the other side."

"Thanks." With a quick backwards glimpse at Rhonyn, he nonchalantly made his way to the copse. Once hidden from view on the other side, he fled deeper into the forest, running like a man possessed.

It wasn't until Rhonyn looked up to check on Conal that he saw him missing, calling out to the woman, "Where is he?"

She hooked a thumb to the copse. "He's in the privy."

Frowning, Rhonyn hesitated between not wanting to give away his intentions and the feeling that Conal was a lot cleverer than anyone gave him credit. "How long's he been there?"

"Not even a minute," she replied, an eyebrow cocked, wondering why he was so interested.

Rhonyn's patience quickly waned and he caught a male bowman's attention and pointed to the copse. "You. Go check on our guest. Make sure he's OK."

The man knitted his brows at the command. "He's probably just takin' a piss. Leave the man in peace."

"Do it," Rhonyn growled.

Rolling his eyes, the man stood and sauntered over to the copse, stopping at the edge. "You OK back there?" When he heard no response or sound, he stepped around then whirled back around. "There's no one here."

Though he had a head start, Conal heard the shouts, which sent a pulse of wild and reckless fear within him. Dodging trees and hurdling fallen logs, he plunged headlong, praying he had enough of a head start that it would take them too long to find his trail, though it wasn't like he was taking care to hide his tracks. He pressed on, swearing he could hear them on his heels. Crashing through a strand of young trees, he grabbed a tree just in time to stop him from falling into a river thirty feet below. Rapidly scanning the terrain, he saw the river was far too wide to leap across, even on a horse. The river had cut a deep channel and the current was quick. Believing he heard them almost here, he inhaled a deep breath and leaped, praying there weren't any rocks below.

His feet felt no bottom and by the time he emerged, the swift current had propelled him well beyond the point of his entrance. The initial shock of the cold water was momentarily forgotten as he turned onto his back to surveil the place where he dove in. Yet no one broke through the trees and a few moments later, the river curved and he was out of sight.

Inhaling a sigh of relief, he turned back around, positioning his feet to his front, letting the river carry him along. Despite the cold water, his adrenaline flowed as he assessed his present situation.

It wasn't as bad as it might appear. He had always lived by his wits and had been in worse scrapes before. He always managed to come out OK. This wasn't any different.

After a while, the current slowed as the river widened and became shallower. All too soon, Conal was forced to stand and walk in mid-calf deep water. The late afternoon sun cast long shadows, but Conal was thankful for the warmth as his soaked clothes clung to his body, chilling him.

Conal trudged along in the river, knowing no one could track him. A half hour later, the river started to narrow and deepen. Soon Conal was again floating, shivering and more than ready to get warm and dry.

Then he saw it, where the river did another bend, a weathered clapboard shack thrust out over the edge of the bank, held up by two pillars made of layered stone. In strong measured strokes, Conal swam to the shack, grabbed hold of a pillar and listened. When sufficient time passed with no sounds, he clambered up the bank and silently stepped onto the deck.

Looking behind him, the path leading to the shack was overgrown indicating no one had been here in quite a while. Pressing the thumb latch on the door, he entered the one room hut. A single shuttered window sat in the middle of the far wall that jutted over the river. In the corner to the left of the door was a small fireplace, a small stack of wood next to it. In the center of the hut was a small table with two chairs. A low pantry chest sat in the right corner next to the door. Above the chest were two shelves, empty except for four pewter mugs. A straw mattress lay on the floor by the window. All were covered with a thin layer of dust.

Conal shivered again and rummaged through the chest and hut, searching for a flint or igniter, finding a flint, striker and tuft down by the wood pile. Having much experience in starting fires, he soon had a fire roaring, his clothes peeled off and draped over the chairs next to the fire.

The grumbling of his stomach reminded him that despite having lunch hours ago, it had been his only meal since yesterday's breakfast. Yet the thought of putting on still wet clothes to search for something to eat was enough to ignore the hunger pains. Once his pants were dry, he would slip out the hut and see if he could find some berries or something else to stave off the appetite.

Standing by the fire, his hands splayed above the warming flames, he glanced down at the brand on his left shoulder, surprised, though not really surprised, that the burnt skin had healed. When he told Rhonyn that he was a fast healer, he was merely relaying what had happened in the past. One time not long after he had joined his first band of outlaws, he had fallen from a roof during an escape and broken his leg. His supposed friends left him there. When the constables came upon him, he had concocted a story that the outlaws had kidnapped him and tossed him off the roof because he was purposely slowing them down. As a bonus, he willingly gave them descriptions of several of the outlaws, even remembering some names they called each other.

They carried him to a barber-surgeon who had set the leg and handed Conal a bill of such an outrageous amount that after his initial shock, he confidently told him that his father had the exchange shop in the market square and if he would be so kind as to take the bill to him. Naturally, the quack's eyes lit up and he bustled out. No sooner had the man left that Conal peeled and chipped off the plaster made of bee wax and sheep lard. By the time he had removed the plaster, the leg had mended.

When he showed up at the outlaw hideout, they were more than surprised, especially knowing he had broken his leg. Eyeing him with overt suspicion, it wasn't long before he decided to move on.

Exhaustion suddenly draped over him and his eyelids became very heavy. Testing his clothes, he was pleased that they had dried and he slipped them back. He then wedged a chair against the front door before stretching out on the straw mattress. A few moments later, he was fast asleep.

Dawn crept over the mountaintops when a kick at the door bolted him awake. A male voice from the outside grumbled, "Put your shoulder into it again. Maybe it's stuck"

"Of course it's stuck, you moron. There's somebody in there," another male voice said. "I smell smoke from a fire."

"Don't call me a moron."

"Well you are. Maybe it's stuck," the voice

imitated. "If it's not locked and it doesn't open what else is it?"

"That still doesn't make me a moron."

"It doesn't take much to make you a moron."

"Spoken like one with experience."

Conal furrowed his brow, concentrating on the voices. He was pretty sure they were male, but there was something about the pitch that was a bit off. Though his first inclination was to leap out the window into the river, the thought of being wet and cold first thing in the morning was unappealing.

He yanked the chair away just as the individual outside thrust a shoulder against the door, sending a dwarf crashing into the table.

"Good morning," Conal cheerily greeted them.

The second dwarf craned his head back to take in the stranger. "Who are you?"

"Name's Conal. This your place?"

"No –" the dwarf replied before being interrupted by the dwarf on the floor who had quickly recovered and stood behind Conal.

"Yes."

"Is it 'no' or 'yes'?" Conal grinned, knowing the truth.

"OK, OK, mebbe it's not ours," the dwarf admitted.

"Your names?"

"I'm Torgreth," the dwarf at the door said with a friendly grin. He was stout like most dwarves, with thick curly long brown hair and a beard that dropped to the middle of his chest. He wore the clothing of a hill dwarf: brown woolen trousers tucked into heavy knee-high leather boots, long-sleeve tan cotton shirt, and a light brown sleeveless tunic of deerskin. He hooked a thumb at the other dwarf. "This is my brother Voldar."

Voldar was about the same height, which was mid-chest on Conal. His hair was a darker brown and his brows thicker and dark, almost black.

"Didn't expect to see anyone here," Torgreth commented.

"I didn't expect to be here."

Voldar glanced around the room then scrunched his face at Conal. "You travel pretty light."

"Long story."

"We got time," Torgreth said, turning around to pick up two very large packs.

"Aren't you two a bit far from home?" Conal prayed they had food in those packs and were feeling generous enough to share some.

The two dwarves exchanged a quick guilty look before Torgreth said, "It's a long story."

"I got time," Conal grinned, causing Torgreth to snort a laugh.

"Then open up the windows and stoke up the fire whilst we set the table."

"We don't got enough," Voldar groused.

"Don't mind him," Torgreth apologized. "Early mornings always make him grumpy." He cast a humorous eye at his brother. "In fact, late mornings make him grumpy as does early and late afternoons… and evenings too."

"What are you blabbering about," Voldar complained, opening up the pack.

"I'm just telling our friend here that you're not the sociable type." He cupped a hand by his face and leaned in to loudly whisper, "Mister Chuckles there doesn't like anyone, so it's nothing personal."

"Will you shut up and help me," Voldar snapped, setting three pewter plates on the table.

Before long, the two dwarves had bread, cheese, and sausage on the table along with bottles of mead. Conal retrieved three mugs and rinsed them out in the river, surveilling the area in the process. Satisfied, he returned to the smell of scrambled eggs.

"You two travel well. I thank you for your hospitality. Hopefully one day I can return the favor."

"Hopefully," Torgreth grinned, ladling eggs onto the plates. "Enjoy."

Needing no urging, Conal scooted a chair out. "So why are you two so far from home?" He sighed in contentment, the food tasting particularly delicious.

"The gist of it is that we got tired of digging," Torgreth explained. "Yeah, we're dwarves and we're supposed to be miners –"

"We're some of the best," Voldar interrupted. "Got noticed by the king himself. But you know what that meant?"

"No?" Conal sipped the mead. Though warmer than he liked, it was still good.

"Meant we had to dig even more. And it's just not digging a dwarf does. It's the carving too. That's what put us off." He suddenly grew morose and plunged a fork into a slice of sausage.

"Dwarves are supposed to be the best carvers in the world," Conal said by way of compliment.

"They are," Voldar huffed. "It's when you ask them to carve totems and strange words and symbols that makes the hair on the back of your neck stand up."

"So we left, sort of snuck away one evening," Torgreth continued. "Been gone ever since."

"They sent someone after us," Voldar sneered. "Didn't even have the guts to send a dwarf. No. They sent a human, no offense."

"None taken. Why would they want you back so badly?"

Voldar paused to study the stranger, suddenly aware that he had already revealed too much.

Sensing his hesitation, Conal sought to reassure him. "While you consider your words, I will reveal why I am here. I had thrown in my lot with a band of highwaymen who decided they no longer needed me and set me up. I was captured and branded."

"Branded?" Torgreth's eyes widened. "You're a runaway slave?"

"No. I was given my freedom shortly after I was branded."

Voldar cocked an eyebrow. "That makes no sense."

Conal explained the attack in the woods and subsequent attachment to Rhonyn's band. "It was when we went back to his assembly point that things went south. There back at the camp was a half-druid."

The two dwarves jerked back like they had been stung. Voldar snapped forward, peering intently into Conal's eyes.

"Was he a tall man? Dark-brown beard and hair,

and eyes the color of coal?"

"Yes."

"By the gods," he wailed, leaping up. "He's found us. Pack everything up. We gotta get out of here." He gulped down the rest of his ale while trying to decide whether to finish eating or toss the food out the window.

"I say we finish eating," Conal calmly spoke

"You can stay here if you like," Voldar replied, wolfing down the breakfast, "but we're going."

"Why? I lost them when I jumped in and floated down the river."

"You don't understand," Voldar said, stuffing everything back in their packs while Torgreth doused the fire. "The druid part is bad enough. That part is still a man and has to sleep. It's the other part that never sleeps, roaming at will."

"You mean like some spirit?"

"Exactly."

"What about when he's awake?"

Voldar paused. "I don't know."

"And I don't want to find out," Torgreth added. "You coming?"

"Might as well."

Voldar pushed the door open and froze, the shadow of the imposing man spreading over him.

"Well look who we found," the half-druid taunted.

CHAPTER 9

Gwen

Gwen's flesh burned with intense heat and a migraine pounded at her skull, threatening to send her into unconsciousness. Her sight was gone, nothing but darkness everywhere she looked. Amidst the swirling pain and confusion, she felt betrayed.

Tobias had tricked her.

She crawled in a circle, trying blindly to backtrack into the mirror, and bumped into something. A hand touched her shoulder and she flinched away.

"What's wrong with her?" Tobias asked. His concerned words echoed oddly as if he were far away.

"You didn't tell me she was a Prestige," another voice said.

"I didn't know she was," Tobias replied.

"She must be. Her body is trying to defend itself from the residual magic of the teleportation."

Gwen heard someone approach her. Despite the worry she heard in Tobias's voice, the sting of betrayal was still present. She assumed the other voice was Eradore, but he sounded insane. She was no wizard.

"Take a deep breath," the assumed Eradore said. "Focus on the sound of my voice."

Gwen tried to do as he asked, but the pounding migraine made it almost impossible. "I can't," she gasped.

"Hand me the bowl with the mint in it," Eradore said. "It's on that shelf." There was a pause.

"Which one is that?" Tobias asked.

Eradore made a scoffing sound in his throat. "It's the third bowl from the right."

A moment later, the strong smell of mint mixed with something less desirable stung Gwen's nostrils. She gagged, but the pain in her head quickly faded.

"Now can you focus?" Eradore asked her.

Gwen's vision was still dark, but she turned her head in the direction of his voice. "Yes," she replied.

"Good, now listen carefully. Within the darkness of your mind, there are runes. Point your mental gaze toward your inner self and focus on the first rune that you see."

"I don't understand what any of that means," Gwen said.

Eradore gave a frustrated sigh and muttered something about humans and magic. "Let's try something else. Stare straight ahead and envision a mirror before you. What do you see?"

"I see a shadowy figure wearing a crown."

"Interesting," Eradore whispered. "Focus on the figure."

Gwen did so, and suddenly her viewpoint changed. It was as if she rushed up to the mirror and exchanged places with the shadow. She looked out into the blackness and saw faint glowing symbols floating around. She fixated on the nearest one. It was flowing and had many curves, yet at the same time it resembled an animal, a bird. It reminded Gwen of a dove.

She wanted to say that she found one, but she was afraid she'd lose her focus on the rune. Instead, she nodded her head slowly, hoping that Eradore would understand the movement.

"Speak the name of the rune," Eradore told her.

As she was wondering how he expected her to do that, the word formed in her mouth and she said, "*Bunús*."

An invisible force inside her aligned with her spine, straight and taut. The burning of her skin stopped and her vision returned. She was on all fours and the face of an elf was staring back at her. His flesh was tan, his hair a honey-brown hue. Piercing blue eyes watched her intently.

"What happened to me?" Gwen asked, pushing herself into a sitting position.

"Tobias failed to mention your magical inclination, which caused issues with your body. Most wizards have defensive spells woven into their portals. It keeps enemy wizards from entering their domains."

"I'm not a wizard," Gwen said.

"Not yet," Eradore clarified. "But you will be. These things take time."

"No, I mean I don't have magical powers. And I don't want to be a wizard, anyway."

"Have you ever cast a spell?" Eradore asked.

"No."

"Then how do you know you don't want to be a wizard?"

Gwen was silent, unsure of how to answer. She

looked at Tobias, who shrugged. "I'm not here to talk about magic," Gwen said, turning back to Eradore. "I'm here to talk about rescuing my father."

Eradore stood and turned his attention to Tobias. "Let us discuss this opportunity you mentioned, then we will talk about magic. Does that please everyone?"

"That works for me," Tobias replied.

Eradore looked back at Gwen.

"Yes," she answered.

Tobias helped Gwen to her feet and they followed Eradore through a door that led to a curved terrace. There was a sitting area protected from the sun by a long awning that stretched out from the side of what Gwen realized was a tower. She peered over the side of the railing and saw a city sprawled out below them.

"Where are we?" she asked, cutting off Tobias and Eradore's conversation. "Sorry," she added, frowning, and took a seat.

"It's all right," Eradore replied. "We're still in Penshaw. This tower is my home, but this portion of it does not exist in the seen world."

Gwen blinked, the explanation going over her head.

"What he means is that if you were standing in the street down there and looked at this place, you would only see part of the tower," Tobias explained. "The rest is hidden by magic."

"Can other wizards see it?" Gwen asked.

"It's possible, though highly improbable," Eradore answered. "Why do you ask?"

"The men that are chasing us … Tobias thinks they are using magic to track us."

"Ah, yes. The men you speak of have a sorcerer with them. He's using an item that belongs to one of you to keep track of your location."

"How do you know?" Gwen asked.

"There is little that escapes my notice," Eradore replied vaguely.

Gwen didn't like his answer and asked another question. "Any idea why they are following us all this way over a stolen horse?"

"That will take some digging," Eradore said. "I have some people looking into it as we speak."

"I thought we agreed to talk about magic after?" Tobais asked, looking at Gwen and raising his brows questioningly.

"Yes, I'm sorry. I have a lot on my mind." Gwen cast her gaze back down at the city.

"That's understandable, but we must sort one thing at a time," Eradore said. "Firstly, you said Boris was captured. Where did the king's men take him?"

"To the outpost outside Dawsbury," Tobias answered. "Him and several others were chained and taken prisoner."

"What are you asking for?"

"Enough men to raid the outpost and rescue the prisoners. We need members of the rebellion who don't mind spilling blood, because we're going to make a statement with this attack."

A grin tugged at the corner of Eradore's mouth but he remained silent for a moment. Gwen turned her attention to the elf. He wore pale blue robes that were thin and loose-fitting. Gwen thought she could see the material shimmer every so often, but figured she was seeing things.

"It's risky," Eradore finally said.

"It is," Tobias confirmed. "Gwen wants to see her father freed before she'll throw in with us."

A knowing look passed between the two men and Gwen pretended not to notice, but her curiosity was piqued. There was something more going on and she was determined to find out what it was.

"I'll send word through the city," Eradore said. "We'll gather men and weapons. Do you want to take the lead on this?"

"No," Tobias replied. "I don't think I'm ready to lead men into battle yet."

"Most leaders are never ready to lead. Moments like this are thrust upon them, and they do what is needed. Regardless, I'll put Roland in charge. You'll be his second in command."

"I can handle that. There's one more thing. Gwen wants to help free Boris."

Eradore looked at Gwen. She returned his stare.

"It's not safe," the elf said. "I'd prefer that you stay here."

"I won't," Gwen replied, her tone defensive.

"I'm not going to force you to stay, I was merely stating my opinion. You are free to go if you want, but I think there are far more pressing matters to deal with."

"Such as what?"

"Your training," Eradore said.

"I told you, I don't have any interest in being a wizard."

"We don't choose the magic. It chooses us."

"It can choose someone else, because I don't want it," Gwen huffed.

Eradore laughed, a melodic sound. "I'm afraid it doesn't work that way. Now that you have given life to the *bunús,* you will become aware of magical things. It's important that you learn to control your power, lest you hurt those around you."

"What is a *bunús?*" Gwen asked. At the mention of the word, she felt something pulse against her spine. It wasn't painful, just … different. It was akin to a muscle spasm.

"You felt it, didn't you?" Eradore smiled. "You'll get used to it."

"What is it?" Gwen repeated.

"It is like a key to a door, the door being you. You are a vessel, and the *bunús* opens you to the magic outside of yourself. With time and practice, you will see life in a different way, a *better* way."

Gwen wasn't so sure about that, but she was becoming more curious as Eradore explained things. If this magic could help rescue her father, then maybe it was something she should explore. That, and if she was going to join Tobias and Eradore in their quest to overthrow the king, the more she had at her disposal, the better.

"What can you teach me?" Gwen asked.

Eradore looked at Tobias. "Go seek out Roland. He's probably at the brothel on Desire Street, the Canary. I'll get word spreading to the others."

"As you wish," Tobias said, his excitement obvious. He rose from his chair and looked at Gwen. "I'll be back soon. You're in good hands with Eradore. Listen to what he has to say. You might change your mind."

"I doubt it," Gwen said, but as Tobias left, she felt like she was on the verge of making a decision already.

"The first thing we need to determine is what kind of magic user you are."

"There are different kinds of wizards?" Gwen asked.

"Anyone who can use magic is called a Prestige. Wizards are at the top in terms of power. They are the rarest type of Prestige and can do things most people can't fathom."

"That's what you are?"

Eradore nodded. "Yes. Sorcerers are people who can summon magic, but they require spell components. The items needed depend upon the type of spell and sorcerers can only memorize a certain number of spells. The more powerful the sorcerer, the more spells they can retain."

Gwen was afraid his explanation was going to take a while, and she wanted to avoid being bored. "How many types of Prestiges are there?" she asked.

"Three," Eradore replied. "The last type are mages. They are able to summon certain abilities through the runes they gather. Some abilities you'll learn on your own, but most of them will require someone to teach you. Once you've gained a rune, it will be displayed on your flesh."

"What do you mean displayed on my flesh? Like a tattoo?"

"No, like a brand. The rune will burn itself into

your skin."

"Where?" Gwen asked, getting worried.

"It depends on what the rune does. Some mages are able to turn their skin into stone, deflecting arrows. A mark like that would appear on the chest, most likely. Other runes will appear on your hands or feet."

"So, a mage could potentially have their entire bodies covered in these runes?"

"Potentially, yes," Eradore answered. "Though that is really up to the individual. You don't have to take every rune that you find."

Gwen found some relief with that knowledge. The image of her entire body being covered in brands, whether they offered power or not, wasn't something she was keen on. Perhaps that was a bit vain of her to think, but she didn't care.

"How do I know which Prestige I am?" she asked.

"By taking a pilgrimage to the Obsidian Altar."

"A pilgrimage? I can't take time to travel … wherever. How long does it take to get there?"

Eradore snapped his fingers. "We're already here."

CHAPTER 10

Conal

Hearing the half-druid's voice, Conal whirled around and dove through window and into the river below, swimming as low to the bottom as possible, letting the current carry him along. Arrows pierced the water above him. Feet furiously fluttering and his lungs desperate for air, he felt the current sweeping him down river. When he could no longer hold his breath, he popped up, gasped a lungful of air and plunged back down, never bothering to check if they were still there. Yet no arrows drilled into the water.

With the current picking up speed, he prayed he was now far enough downstream to be free of pursuit. Throwing caution to the wind, he raised his head far enough above the water to inhale a deep breath while scanning the riverbanks. His luck held as he saw no one on either side.

Yet the current was beginning to move him along at a faster pace. Deciding he'd had enough of this river, he worked his way towards the left bank, coming upon a bend where the river's course had deposited a layer of sand ankle deep below the surface.

Trudging across the submerged sandbar, Conal scrambled up the gentle slope and stood in the middle of a small meadow getting his bearings. The morning's sun felt good and he peeled off his shirt, twisting it in his hands and wringing out the wetness then laying it out on the grass. His hearing on edge, he listened to the sounds of the gurgling river and leaves rattling in the morning breeze.

Hesitating to take off his boots to let them dry, he decided worst case would be someone coming upon him and him diving back into the river, his clothes left behind. Yanking off boots and trousers and underclothes, he wrung out the clothing and laid them next to the shirt then lay back in the grass, letting the sun dry his body.

After two hours of nerve-wracking imagined sounds, he was ready to move on. The clothes were dry enough to wear, though the leather boots were still damp. Judging from the direction of the sun, the river was meandering south. Conal figured the river's course would eventually lead him to a town, so he worked his way along the edge.

By the midafternoon the forest gave way to farmland. Though still cautious, he decided a stranger traveling the edges of farms would draw more attention than someone walking the main road. Edging the low stone walls bordering a pasture, he scanned both directions before stepping onto the rutted road.

With little traffic on the road, he relaxed, pondering what the next town was and whether he had been there before as a member of Oscon's gang. The area looked vaguely familiar, though in truth so many of these farming communities looked the same.

The road crested and he saw the fortified city in the near distance. A branch of the river he had spent so much time in these past two days ran between a tall circular barbican and the crenelated granite walls. Conal frowned for it did look familiar though it had been a while since he had been here.

Trying to remember the name of the city, a sudden premonition pulsed within and he looked back over his shoulder to see a large group of riders in the far distance cantering towards him, a tall man garbed in huntsman clothing leading the group. Fear gave strength to his legs and he fled up the road. A voice behind him shouted something he couldn't distinguish, but he knew what it was.

They had recognized him.

His legs churning, lungs screaming, he raced for the gates.

The closer he came the more he had to weave around merchant wagons, farmers carrying produce on their backs, children gamboling in and out of traffic, and indifferent soldiers heading out to patrol the surrounding area. Casting a quick furtive glance behind him, he saw them gaining on him.

One soldier connected the approaching riders with the breathlessly fleeing runner and attempted to intercede and question him, only to be stiff armed and knocked down. By the time he jumped up and gave chase, Conal was at the gate. The gate guards, seeing the altercation, stepped in front of him, their halberds crossed.

"Lemme through," Conal pleaded.

"Not so fast," one guard threatened.

"Artek," a voice behind the guards called out. "You made it."

The guard turned to see a handsome, well-built man in merchant's clothing, smiling at Conal. "You know him?"

"Of course I do. He's my cousin." The man pushed his way between the guards, placing an arm across Conal's shoulders. "I hope the trip wasn't too exhausting."

"Good to see you too… cousin."

The indignant guard Conal had stiff armed came fuming up just as Conal turned and pointed at Drustan and Rhonyn now at the edges of the crowds on the road. "Highwaymen. They robbed me."

Startled at the accusation, the guards' attention narrowed on the approaching riders. With their attention diverted, the man propelled Conal past them and bustled him through the barbican and onto the bridge leading to the gate to the city

Conal heard the raised voices, especially one belonging to Rhonyn who cried out, "Stop him. The man's a thief."

"Don't look back. Keep walking," the man urged.

"You there," a guard's voice called out. "You two. Stop. I said 'stop.'"

They were halfway across when the man said, "When I say 'run,' you run. Stay close."

Conal ticked his head, wondering if he was being led into greater trouble.

The man nodded as though responding to something Conal had said, while sliding his eyes to see several guards hustling towards them.

"Run!"

They bolted across the remaining portion of the bridge, Conal doing his best to keep up for despite the merchant's clothing, the man was fast. Once through the gates, the man swerved left, dodging people and livestock with the skill of an acrobat, Conal hard pressed to keep pace. Three intersections later, he ducked right. By the time he slowed the pace to a walk, they had turned left, right, and double-backed so many times that Conal was quite lost.

"Thank you," he said, catching his breath. "I owe you… cousin."

The man grinned. "You looked like a man who needed a friend. What's your name?"

"I am called Conal," he replied with a heartfelt smile.

"I am Bryok. Tell me Conal, why were those men chasing you?"

Conal twisted his head to regard his deliverer. Bryok was half a handspan taller, clean shaved, with silky smooth dark auburn hair tied in a ponytail. He had the face and body that made women look twice and Conal noticed the frequent stares and smiles that he elicited. It was apparent to him at least that the man was not a merchant for he walked with the strut of a warrior, and his eyes were constantly watching, taking everything in.

"It's sort of a long story."

"I'm a patient man, besides… you have someplace else to go?" Bryok chuckled.

"Not really," Conal shrugged.

"When's the last time you ate?" Bryok led them down a side street that emptied onto another side street.

Conal cocked an eyebrow at him. "I'm running for my life and you want to know when I last ate?"

"By the way you were running away from your pursuers and the fact that you have no travel bag in addition to not being from around here, I made the assumption you might like something to eat before you moved on." He stopped below a carved wooden sign of a cleric's head and an ale stein suspended from a metal rod high above a door.

Conal silently read the name drawn in calligraphy on the glazed window in the door, *The Bishop's Head*. Thoughts of a warm meal and a cold ale caused him to salivate. "I had breakfast early this morning with two dwarves."

"Sounds like an interesting start of the day," Bryok acknowledged, opening the door.

In contrast to the bright sunny day outside, the tavern was dark even with the candles on the tables and wall sconces. Conal blinked trying to adjust to the dim light.

Bryok moved with accustomed ease, weaving around tables, patrons, and serving girls to a table in the corner, sitting where he could see who came in the door. Conversations, momentarily paused when he and Conal had entered, resumed at the same levels, the clatter of eating and drinking mixed in.

A pretty serving girl a year or two younger than Conal approached the table, favorably eying the two handsome men. "What'll you have, gentlemen?"

"Meat, cheese, bread if it's fresh and ale that's cold," Bryok replied with a smile.

"Right away." She sashayed back to the kitchen.

"Pretty girl," Bryok commented.

"Yes, she is," Conal agreed, his eyes finally adjusting to the low light.

The tavern had twenty or more tables, half of them occupied mostly with male patrons. The women who sat at the tables were the usual wives, lovers or business partners. Conal noticed a table closer to the door where an attractive older woman dominated the conversation, the men nodding respectfully.

"You were telling me about breakfast with two dwarves," Bryok said. "Where was this?"

Conal waited as the serving girl deposited the two mugs of ale. Lifting the ale in salute, he swallowed a deep satisfying draught, licking his lips. "This is good," he sighed, finally relaxing. "It was… uh… upriver a ways. By the way, where am I? I mean what town is this?"

"Monkreth."

"Ah," he nodded. "Thought I recognized the place. It's been a while."

"You've been here before?"

"Yeah. About two, three years ago."

"What were you doing here?" Bryok frowned, puzzled.

"Uh… let's just say that I was here on, uh… business." He grinned.

"Is that why they were chasing you? Business?"

"Ah, no." Conal paused again as the serving girl placed platters of cold meat, cheese, and warm bread on the table. When she ambled off to another table, he asked, "Why did you stick your neck out for me? You don't even know me."

"Like I said, you looked like a man who needed a friend," he cryptically replied, slicing a piece of cheese. "You were telling me about the two dwarves.”

“Back to the dwarves again, eh? Why do I get the feeling these two dwarves are important to you?”

A middle-aged man with thinning hair sauntered up to their table, hands on hips, staring at Conal. “You look familiar.”

Conal paused mid-bite, returning the gaze, the memory of swindling the man out of 40 gold regals suddenly crystalizing. “You ever been to Hemlyn?” he parried.

“No.”

Conal shrugged and impishly grinned. “I get that a lot, though usually from the ladies, especially the pretty ones and sometimes even the married ones.” He winked knowingly. “I’ve been here before, visiting my cousin.” He ticked his head at Bryok. “I’ve been known to enjoy the company of an attractive lady, but I stay away from the married ones. Too much trouble, if you know what I mean.”

Conal’s answer didn’t seem to satisfy the man. “I’ve had dealings with you. I know I have.”

“I doubt it,” Conal affirmed. “Other than my cousin and the ladies, there’s not much else here that interests me.”

Recognition swept through the man and he thrust a finger at Conal. “I remember you now. It was almost three years ago. I don’t forget a face, especially of a man who swindled me.”

“You’ve made a mistake,” Bryok interrupted, his eyes flashing. “Why don’t you go back to your table and let us dine in peace.”

“Not on your life,” the man fumed. “I’m

reporting the both of you to the authorities." He stood full height, folding his arms in self-righteousness.

"That would be a grave error," Bryok replied, his voice cold and hard. "I will ask you one more time to leave us alone."

"Ha," the man sniffed in derision. "I know my rights and I know that man is a thief. And you're probably one too."

He started to turn when Bryok's hand shot out and grabbed the man by the wrist, causing him to waver and grunt in pain. "Why don't you sit down with us."

Conal scooted over an empty chair from the nearby table as Bryok guided the man to sitting.

The man's face turned ashen and his lips quivered when his eyes abruptly glazed over.

"You need to finish quickly," Bryok warned.

"I'm done," Conal answered, downing the last of his ale.

The serving girl came up, smiling at Conal and Bryok then looked at the man. "What's wrong with him?"

"He's fine," Bryok said, "just a little over come with the news that his sister died."

"O how horrible," the serving girl commiserated. "The poor man."

"Give him a few minutes. He'll be fine." He placed several coins on the table adding a generous tip.

The girl's eyes lit up. "Thank you." Looking directly at Conal, she lowered her voice and said, "I'm Brigit. Come back real soon."

Conal smiled, wishing he could but knowing it would be a long time before he set foot in Monkreth again.

"C'mon, cousin," Bryok urged. "We have places to go."

Once outside, Conal asked, "How'd you do that?"

"Magic," Bryok chuckled then held up his hand displaying a small inverted ring on the tip of his middle finger. Flipping the hand over revealed a small sharp barb. "It's coated with a numbing drug. When I grabbed his arm, I made sure the tip punctured the vein in his wrist. It works very quickly." He started walking. "It'll last long enough to us to get out of here."

"Where're we going?" Conal's senses were again on edge, as though they were being watched.

"I've got a place close by where we can sequester ourselves for a day or two. Now tell me about the two dwarves."

"What is it with the dwarves?" Conal demanded.

"Just answer the question," Bryok snapped. "Sorry. There's a lot happening and you may be stuck in the middle of something you have no idea about." He turned down an alley.

Conal shook his head. Nothing made a whole lot of sense these past few days. "Their names were Torgreth and –"

"Voldar," Bryok answered with an exasperated breath, "which means Drustan probably already has them."

Conal stutter-stepped at the name. "You know

Drustan?"

"Yes. He's my brother."

Conal sucked in a breath. "He's a half-druid." As soon as he said it, a terrible foreboding filled him. He shifted a look at Bryok whose attention remained focused forward. "Does that mean…"

"Yes. I am also a half-druid."

CHAPTER 11

Gwen

Gwen looked over the railing and the city of Penshaw was gone. In its place was a sight unlike anything she'd ever seen before. Where the city had been far below, this place was level with the terrace. White marble floors and walls created a massive empty space except for the black altar that stood in the center.

"Where are we?" Gwen asked, awed.

"This is the Chamber of the Altar," Eradore answered. "And that," he pointed a slender hand, "is the Obsidian Altar. This is a sacred place among Prestige. This is where every Prestige begins their path. They come here to learn of themselves. Once you know where your path leads, you can fully embrace the magic."

Movement caught Gwen's attention and she spotted a few people, mostly human, walking through the chamber. There was an elf among them, but he was quiet and aloof while the humans chatted amicably.

"Do you want to know who you truly are?" Eradore asked.

Gwen stared at the altar, struggling internally. Just a short time ago, she was serving the patrons of her father's inn. Now, she was with a strange elf in an even stranger place contemplating becoming a

Prestige. She still wasn't quite sure what that meant, but the mystery was alluring. The image of the shadowy figure wearing a crown flashed in her mind, and she turned her gaze from the altar to Eradore.

"I do, but I'm afraid," Gwen said.

"Afraid of what?"

"I'm afraid of what I might find out about myself. I'm not sure I'm ready for things to change so drastically."

Eradore leaned forward, and Gwen caught the aroma of woodland scents. Trees, flowers, and an earthy smell that reminded her of freshly plowed farming ground all swirled together, adding to the exoticness of the elf.

"Change comes whether we want it to or not," Eradore said softly. "We can embrace it, or we can fight it. I've lived long enough that I've learned the latter brings only pain and heartache. Come, let us see what Prestige you are."

Eradore walked around the table and offered Gwen his hand. She accepted it and stood, doubt still tugging at her mind. The railing vanished before her eyes, and Eradore stepped down onto the marble floor. Gwen followed and released his hand but remained close to his side. They walked slowly toward the altar, and Gwen's heart began pounding within her chest.

When they were a few paces away, Gwen stopped. Eradore turned to her, his face expressionless. Gwen wondered how the elf was able to mask his emotions so well, but the thought was quickly drowned in the deluge of her anxiety. Eradore waited patiently until Gwen worked up the nerve to continue. She inhaled deeply and closed the distance to the altar.

"How does this work?" Gwen asked. Sitting atop the altar, she spotted a polished dagger that looked like it was forged of silver and immediately regretted asking.

"The altar requires blood. Not much," Eradore added, seeing Gwen's face pale. "Just a small amount. You'll cut your palm and touch the altar. The rest is different for everyone, but you will know which Prestige you are."

Gwen looked at the dagger. It was clean, not a trace of any blood or finger smudges on the hilt. The altar, too, was devoid of anything that would imply its purpose. Gwen was nervous, but her curiosity prevailed. She gingerly grabbed the dagger and pressed the tip against her palm. Her hand was trembling, but Eradore laid his hand on hers, steadying it. His touch helped calm her. She drew a breath and held it.

In a quick movement, she pressed the blade hard against her skin and slashed down, slicing a gash down the middle. Her flesh spread apart and blood welled within the wound. Gwen hissed in pain and touched the top of the altar. She saw Eradore touch the side of the altar before a vision engulfed her.

Someone screamed, and Gwen turned to look.

She was rooted in place, her hand attached to the altar, but she saw the carnage. Bodies littered a long hallway, pools of blood growing beneath them all. A figure disappeared into a doorway and there was another scream, this one a man. Despite her desire to flee, Gwen couldn't avert her eyes. The scenery moved around her of its own accord, and suddenly she was standing in the doorway.

A man wearing a crown was crumpled on the floor, clutching at his wounded neck. Blood spurted between his fingers, staining his garments and his hand. Another man stood over him, a sword held tightly in his grasp. It was evident that the one standing was the culprit of the grisly crime.

"Long live the king," the man sneered. He stiffened suddenly and turned around. His face was masked by moving shadows, but Gwen was certain the man could clearly see her. "You!" he exclaimed with disbelief. A blue outline began to glow off the man, though he seemed oblivious to it. He stepped toward her, but the scenery pulled her away and began to fade. Before the vision was gone completely, Gwen spotted a woman among the bodies in the hall also wearing a crown.

Gwen blinked and exhaled slowly, not sure what to make of what she'd seen. Eradore was staring at her.

"You're the …" He paused, then said, "… a mage."

"How do you know?"

"Look at me. What do you see?"

"An elf?" Gwen said quizzically.

"Look closer," Eradore replied. "Do you see anything out of the ordinary?"

Gwen squinted, but that didn't help. Then she noticed it. A faint glow around him, this one green.

"I see a green light," she said, but that explanation didn't seem right. "Well, not a light, but something glowing."

Eradore smiled. "You have the gift of Sight," he said. "All mages have it. The color you see is called the Aspect. Everyone gives it off, but no one is sure of its purpose."

"Who were those people in the vision?" Gwen asked.

Eradore shrugged. "Who knows?"

"Were they real? Did that slaughter really happen?"

"It's possible, but we can't know for certain. The altar the vision gives is different for everyone. Some people see loved ones and others see things that have no meaning at all. The important thing is that we now know what you are. A mage."

Eradore was looking past Gwen at something behind her. She looked over her shoulder and spotted a black-haired man that gave her chills. He was flanked by three soldiers on either side, and they were heavily armed.

"What is the meaning of this?" Eradore demanded as they approached.

Gwen looked the man up and down. His clothing looked expensive. A navy shirt was tucked into black pants, and his boots shone with fresh polish. The man wore a flowing purple cape as well, and the gold clasps on his shoulders were fashioned into the shape of wolf heads. It was obvious to Gwen that the man viewed himself as important. His demeanor was borderline pompous.

"By order of His Majesty, the Chamber is now closed and off limits. Please disperse immediately or suffer the consequences."

Eradore stepped past Gwen and intercepted the man. "King Torian holds no sway over this domain," the elf said.

"He does now." The man retrieved a scroll case from one of the soldiers and withdrew a rolled parchment. He unfurled it and held it out for Eradore to see. Gwen's mother had taught her to read at an early age, and she scanned the flowing script. It detailed how the king had revoked the treaty with the Order, and the Chamber of the Altar was now property of the crown. At the bottom was the signature of the king and a stamp with his emblem.

"Torian goes too far," Eradore said.

"That's *King* Torian," the man retorted. "Now take your servant girl and leave this place before I have you arrested."

Gwen could tell by the anger on Eradore's face that he wanted to say something more, but instead he spun around and grabbed her hand, tugging her along back to the terrace of the tower. They crossed the threshold, and Gwen glanced back at the man. He stared after her, his gaze haunting her even after Eradore snapped his fingers and the Chamber disappeared.

"Who was that?"

"That was Viktor," Eradore replied. "He's one of Grimmar the Mage-Breaker's lackeys."

"Mage-Breaker? That sounds ominous," Gwen said.

"Given what just transpired, it will be soon. He hates magic and those who practice it. I'm certain he's behind this move. The king has never taken issue with us before." Eradore stared off at nothing for a moment, and his face became devoid of any emotion. "No matter. The Order is likely dealing with the situation already."

"What's the Order?"

"It is the governing body of the Prestiges. There's a hierarchy of leadership, but it's mainly for show. Most Prestiges live solitary lives, but there are a few who serve their communities or hold positions of power within the court. I suspect that's about to change. I'm sorry to overwhelm you with these things, but it took me by surprise. Please, let's get back to the task at hand."

"All right. You said I'm a mage?" Gwen asked.

"Yes. Now that you have the Sight, you can see people's Aspects."

"How many colors are there? The man in the vision had blue and yours is green. That's two, at least."

"Each race has the same color. Human Aspects are blue, elves are green, and dwarves are brown. There are others, but those are the main ones you'll see."

"Can I stop seeing the Aspects? It's a little odd seeing colors coming off people."

"Unfortunately, no. You'll get used to it with time. Most mages don't even notice the Aspects after a while. It becomes normal."

Gwen was disappointed to hear that, but it was too late to change her mind now. She peered over the railing and saw the city again. Dusk was beginning to creep over the landscape and Gwen looked at Eradore, puzzled.

"It was mid-afternoon when Tobias and I got here. It looks like it's getting dark now. Is that some sort of illusion?"

"No. Traversing vast distances by magic makes travel quicker, but the time still passes normally. Perhaps we should take a break to eat, then we can continue."

"How much is there to cover?" Gwen asked.

"I can only provide the basics, since you are a mage. Magic works too differently for me to train you, and I can't see runes. There is a mage here in Penshaw that is part of the rebellion. She can show you your first rune, but if you want more of them, you'll have to seek out other mages."

"First things first," Gwen said. "We need to rescue my father and the others from the outpost. When he's safe, I'll decide what I want to do."

Over the next hour, the two ate a meal and Eradore showed Gwen some of his spell books. She couldn't read the magical texts, but he explained in more detail how magic worked for him. Once darkness fell and Tobias had yet to return, Eradore showed Gwen to a room where she could spend the night.

"We have a room at the inn," Gwen told the elf, but he shook his head.

"It's safer for you to stay in the tower. The soldiers can't track you here, and there's no telling what else Grimmar is plotting now that he's got the king's ear in his hand."

Gwen's stomach was full, and she was getting sleepy, so she didn't argue. Eradore retired to his own room and Gwen climbed into bed, stretching out on the comfortable feather mattress. She yawned and closed her eyes, only intending to rest them for a moment.

The next thing she knew, Eradore was looking down at her. Morning light filtered in through the room's sole window and the elf smiled.

"I've sent word to Aimil. She's coming here to meet you."

"Who's Aimil?" Gwen asked, rubbing the sleep from her eyes.

"She's the mage I told you about. I've also heard from Tobias."

"Is everything all right?" Gwen sat up, worry for Tobias's safety forcing her wide awake.

"He's fine," Eradore replied. "But I have some bad news. Our spies at the outpost say that the prisoners have been tortured. Boris isn't doing well."

CHAPTER 12

Conal

Conal's heart skipped a beat and his eyes roamed the surrounding doors and alleyways for a route to escape.

"You do not need to fear me," Bryok reassured him. "I am not like my brother."

"How do I know that?" Conal retorted.

"You don't. You'll have to trust me." He turned right into an alleyway and stopped when Conal didn't follow. "You can take your chances on your own or you can let me help you. I will not force you." He continued on down the alleyway.

His mind racing, Conal knew he wouldn't last on his own with Drustan looking for him. And once the man in the tavern spilled the news that he was in the city, it would be even harder. Noting that Bryok hadn't bothered to wait for him, Conal decided he was his best option at the moment. Jogging to catch up, Conal matched strides with him.

"How do you know I'm not leading you back to Drustan?"

"I don't, but at least you fed me."

Bryok chuckled. "Let's hope your friend in the tavern decides it's not worth the effort to search for you." Stopping before a nondescript door, he quickly glanced up and down the alley before opening the door. Once inside, he turned and bolted the door and placed a crossbeam across it. "Makes it hard to get in."

"And almost as hard to get out," Conal pointed out.

"I have other ways of getting out."

"Figured."

Bryok led him through the dark interior hallway to a set of stairs then up two dimly lit flights to a door midway down the hall. Silently opening the door, he locked it behind them and slid a crossbeam into the holders.

The room was inky dark until Bryok held up a glow crystal that revealed an empty room with four hallways leading away.

"Follow me."

Bryok headed to the second hallway on the left. "This place is all interconnected, so it's easy to get lost, sometimes even when you know where you are."

Conal frowned, puzzling out how one could be lost if he knew where he was?

At the end of the hallway, a spiral staircase descended. Without hesitation, Bryok curved around with the steps, the light lowering with each step, Conal close on his heels. After a far longer time than it took going up two flights, the stairs emptied into another large dark empty room with more hallways.

"This is crazy," Conal complained. "Where are we?"

"Patience, my young friend. We're almost there." Bryok took the second hallway to the right this time.

By the time they reached the solid oak door at the end, Conal swore they had to be somewhere far beyond the city walls. Past the door was another set of spiral stairs that led up.

"How much farther?" Conal huffed.

"Top of the stairs."

Several minutes later, they emerged onto a platform surrounded by solid granite. Conal watched as Bryok pressed a stone and a section of the wall swung open, light from a fireplace spilling through the opening.

"Where are we?" Conal gazed around the spacious room, the walls carved from stone.

"We are inside the mountain behind the city."

Bryok retrieved a taper near the fireplace and walked around the room lighting sconces and candelabras, revealing a room far larger than Conal's first impression. Except for a wide ornate desk near the fireplace, a reading chair close by, and several bookshelves against the walls, the room was devoid of any decoration or personal touch. A single door adorned the wall to the right of the fireplace.

"You live here?"

"Yes."

Conal walked around the room, nearly stumbling over a small chest by the desk. Skirting the chest, he pointed to the door. "I assume that leads to the kitchen, bedroom and other rooms?"

"I don't cook," Bryok grinned. "But yes, there is a sort of kitchen… and other rooms. But let's get down to business, shall we?" He scooted out the chair behind the desk and sat. "Tell me why my brother was chasing you."

"I thought you wanted to know about the

dwarves." Conal sat in the reading chair.

"Now that I know their names, I know all I need to know."

"Like what?"

Bryok studied him a moment then relented. "I suppose it's only right that you know, now that you're involved. Torgreth and Voldar are brothers, as you probably already surmised. They are from the dwarf kingdom of Gurim-duhr. They are master stonecutters and carvers, probably the best at their craft."

"Those two?" Conal scoffed. "How can that be? They're too young."

"How old do you think they are?" Bryok said.

"Probably my age."

"Try doubling that, maybe even tripling it."

"What?" Conal's jaw dropped. "That's impossible. I've seen dwarves before and they don't look like they're in their fifties."

Bryok shook his head. "I don't know your experience with dwarves, but dwarves live longer than humans. And then there is the little consideration of what they were carving."

Conal knitted his brows and he recalled what Voldar had said. *It's when you ask them to carve totems and strange words and symbols that makes the hair on the back of your neck stand up.* "What were they carving?"

In a calm quiet voice, Bryok said, "Rorkyn Orefell, the King of Gurim-duhr has fallen under the spell of the silken tongue of Havyrd."

"Who's he?"

"Havyrd is a devoted acolyte of Grimmar the

Mage-Breaker."

"Grimmar the Mage-Breaker? Who's he?" Conal scrunched his face hoping he wasn't expected to remember any of this.

"He's the advisor to King Torian. Grimmar is named the Mage-Breaker because he has been relentless in tracking down and killing anyone even suspected of being a mage or having any magic skills. The truth is that he only kills those he can't control. Those willing or forced to submit themselves to him are rune branded."

"Rune branded?" Conal was suddenly aware the Cobra brand on his upper arm.

"I'll explain about runes in a bit. Grimmar needed someone who could carve runes and totems without understanding what they meant. That's where the two dwarves, Voldar and Torgreth, come in. At first, Rorkyn was fine with them carving runes, never suspecting the runes were incantations. But then he got curious as to what the runes said and asked Grimmar about them. Immediately recognizing he had a problem, Grimmar sent Havyrd to work his influence over the king. Havyrd's gift, his power, is his voice. Few can withstand the lull and enticement of his words. Once he focuses his attention on you, you are powerless and will do what he commands. That is what happened to King Rorkyn. Though king, the man is consumed with the mundane, the trivial and the unnecessary. Havyrd actually rules, using the king as a puppet."

Conal pondered the story. "So what does that have to do with me?"

"That's what I want to know. Let's get back to why was my brother chasing you?"

Conal shook his head. "To be honest, I haven't the faintest idea. All I remember is him clasping my hand and the pain nearly killing me. Then when I tell him I was branded –"

"You're branded?" Bryok stiffened.

"Yeah. I got a cobra burnt into my left arm. Here, I'll show you." Conal peeled off his shirt and twisted his body to display the brand.

Bryok suddenly grew somber. "How long ago was this?"

Conal blinked in thought, surprised at how much had happened in between now and the branding. "Yesterday."

"Yesterday?" Bryok exclaimed. "That's impossible. The brand is healed." He frowned as he narrowed his gaze at the cobra head. "How did they brand you? This looks like a tattoo on top of a brand."

Puzzled, Conal bent his head to stare at his shoulder. To his surprise, the cobra head had color interwoven in the design. "That's weird. It wasn't like that last night."

"You say this happened yesterday?" Bryok asked, his disbelief obvious.

"Yeah. If you don't believe me, you can ask Lord Phayrl. He's the one who had me branded."

"Perhaps we should start from the beginning," Bryok said. "Tell me what happened."

Conal related the incidents from the time of the betrayal and his capture to the present. "Now you know as much as I do."

Bryok stood and began pacing, his hands clasped behind him. "So they admitted they were looking for the king's son and they suspected you might be him."

"Yeah," Conal sniffed. "I don't know what they were drinking, but the whole idea is absurd from the start. I know my parents. They live in Urve. I know what I've been doing these past twenty plus years, especially these last years with Oscon, the scum."

Bryok stopped pacing. "May I try something?"

Conal cocked an eyebrow. "Is it going to hurt?"

"Uh… maybe a little."

"What're you gonna do?"

"Clasp you hand like Drustan did."

"Not on your life," Conal loudly objected, shaking his head. "The last time was like the mother of all pain. It hurt worse than hell."

"But it's the only way I can determine the truth."

"What truth?" Conal folded his arms across his chest, his fists hidden.

"The eagle will bear the vipers in its claws, yet from the west a cobra will rise and strike down the eagle."

Conal glared at him. "What the heck does that mean?"

Bryok stood by the chair, gazing down at him. "It is the prophecy of our future. The eagle is the king of Isentol. The vipers are the children of the rightful king returned to reclaim the throne. That the eagle has the vipers in its claws means the children will be captured and powerless against the king until the cobra, whoever he or she is, defeats the king."

Conal blinked at him wondering what he had gotten himself into this time. "I still don't understand what this has to do with me."

"You have a cobra on your shoulder."

"So do lots of other folks."

"You are from the west."

"So are thousands of others."

"You're healing is beyond magical."

"Ah… OK, ya got me there," Conal sighed. "It still doesn't mean I'm some sort of conquering hero. Besides, I'm a lover, not a fighter."

"Self-image a little inflated?" Bryok smirked.

"Very funny." Conal cocked his head to the side. "By the way, what happens when you find this guy?"

"I protect him."

"So Drustan is chasing me because he wants to protect me?" Conal cocked an eyebrow in obvious doubt.

Bryok sat and leaned back. "I find that puzzling too. The only way I can find out is to see what he saw."

"How do you do that?"

"Hand clasp. It lets me connect to your memory."

"Uh-uh. We've been over this ground already. Besides, what will my memory tell you?"

"I don't know until I see. I can plumb the depths to see you earliest memories, some of which you don't know you have. But I can only do that via touch."

"Yeah, well, think of another way. Shouldn't

there be someone who can vouch for what happened? Surely the kid wasn't sent away with no one knowing he was the king's son. Otherwise, he could grow up being a vagabond or a highwayman or a merchant or something quite un-royalty-like. And no one, not even him, would know it."

Bryok pointed to the papers scattered across his desk then to the books on the bookshelves. "There are signs and hints, but one has to study and discern. I am not the only one looking for the son. King Torian has his own wizards and scholars searching the writings and scouring the land tracking you down."

Conal's brow furrowed. "So in other words, if someone thinks I'm the one, my life is over."

"Yes and no," Bryok replied. "Yes, if you decide to go off on your own without protection. King Torian will want you dead, and not just you. He will destroy everyone who he suspects might even remotely be you or associated with you."

"So I'm pretty much screwed anyway I look at it." His jaw clenched.

"Sadly, yes, for the moment. Will you let me determine the truth?"

Conal chewed his lip. "How long will it last?"

"It shouldn't take too long."

"That's not an answer. 'Not too long' is relative."

"The sooner we try it, the quicker we can decide what to do."

Heaving a frustrated and resigned sigh, Conal stuck out his hand, bracing for the pain as Bryok grasped it. At first nothing happened and his guard dropped. Then the pain exploded and he gritted his teeth, his body squirming in the chair, tears flowing down his cheeks. Just as he raised his other hand to pry the grips loose, Bryok let go.

Gasping for breath, he lifted his head to see a smile curl the corners of Bryok's mouth. "Well?"

"I have found you, my Lord."

"That's not funny," Conal snapped.

"It's not meant to be funny. It's true. You are the king's son." Bryok heaved a sigh of satisfaction. "I've been searching for years and years to find you. I can't believe you fell right into my lap. Of all the places I've been to, you end up here."

Finally recovered, Conal dismissively shook his head. "You sure you got this right? Shouldn't I feel sort of revelation, like 'O my God, I'm the long-lost Prince."

"It doesn't work that way. In time, you will come to accept it."

Bryok turned away, exhaling a slow sigh, silently chastising himself for the lie. The truth was he could only see so far back. There was a wall well before the birth-mind. The memories he did see were of a harbor town and his father and mother. Yet by all rights, with the power of the memory-probe, he should be dead. That in itself was enough to give him pause. But was it proof? That he had the strength to endure death-dealing pain along with his magical healing ability surely pointed to him as the one.

But he bore the mark of the cobra.

So which one was he – the king's son or the man who defeats Torian and claims the kingdom as his own? Maybe he was neither. Regardless, until Bryok was sure, he knew he had to keep Conal safe… until he didn't need him anymore.

CHAPTER 13

Gwen

"We have to launch the attack now," Gwen demanded.

Eradore raised his hands placatingly. "We're working on it. Roland and Tobias have gathered enough men to overtake it, but I want you to have a rune before you go. If you are a quick learner, you'll be on your way to the outpost before midday."

"My father could be dead by then."

"You could die if you go to the outpost without some form of protection," Eradore replied calmly.

"I can carry a sword," Gwen said, but she knew he was right.

"Can you wield one? Have you learned to fight against trained soldiers?"

Gwen recognized she was on the losing end of the debate and sighed. "No. I've never even held one before. Well, one time I did, but it was to move it off a table at my father's inn."

"I rest my case," Eradore said. "I know it is difficult, but try to be patient. We will rescue Boris, but everything must be in place."

"It's risky, I get it," Gwen huffed.

"That's not all. The rebellion isn't strong enough to face the king's forces head-on. We must be strategic, calculating. Any loss we suffer will push us further back than we already are."

"Fine. I'll wait for Aimil, and when I've gained

the rune, we go."

"Agreed." Eradore made an odd gesture with his hand, and a pile of folded clothes appeared on the bed beside Gwen. "I've taken the liberty of getting you some new garments."

"What's wrong with these ones?" Gwen asked, brow furrowed. Eradore opened his mouth to speak, then closed it. He lifted a finger into the air and opened his mouth again, then frowned.

"I'm kidding," Gwen said. "These ones are dirty and I feel disgusting."

The hint of a smile pulled at Eradore's lips. "Funny. You can use the bathing chamber to clean up. It's on the floor below this one. When you're done, we'll have breakfast, and then Aimil should be here."

Gwen was relieved to hear that she could get clean and headed straight for the bathing chamber after Eradore left. She took her new clothes with her and set them on a side table. There was a wooden basin filled with water, and Gwen dipped a finger into it. To her surprise, the water wasn't cold. She stripped her dirty clothes off and climbed into the tub.

As much as Gwen wanted to relax in the water and forget her problems, there was too much going on. She felt guilty for not already going to free her father, but she couldn't take on an outpost on her own. Not yet, anyway. If what Eradore said about magic was true, then she could gain the power she needed to stop any injustice.

Gwen got out of the basin and dried off with a long cloth, then put on the clothes Eradore had given her. The black pants were soft and felt like silk, but the material was thick and clung tightly to her skin. The shirt was also black, but it was loose fitting. There was something about the shirt that made her skin tingle, and she made a note to ask Eradore about it.

When she returned upstairs, Eradore was sitting on the terrace with a dark-haired woman that Gwen assumed was Aimil.

"Ah, here she is," Eradore said as Gwen joined them. "Aimil, this is Gwen."

Gwen's eyes widened when she looked upon Aimil. Runes were branded from her wrists up the length of her arms, disappearing under the short sleeves of her leather armor. There were runes on her face as well, one under each of her eyes. Every rune was completely unique from the others. Gwen took a seat at the table and tried not to stare.

"It's nice to meet you," Aimil said. "Eradore says you have some hesitancy about being a mage."

"A little," Gwen admitted.

"I've been where you are, so I can relate. It was long ago, but I remember the emotions like it was only yesterday."

Gwen assumed Aimil was around her own age, just past twenty-two years. Her hair was brown and her skin as dark as night. The branded runes looked like scars, but Gwen didn't find them as abrasive looking as she imagined. The more she studied Aimil's arms, the more she started to like the runes.

"We're getting ready to strike the outpost outside Dawsbury," Eradore said.

"Truly?" Aimil asked, surprised.

"Yes. I confess it's a little premature, but Boris and a few other members of the rebellion are imprisoned. They're too valuable to lose, and Gwen is Boris's adopted daughter."

"Tobias said the same thing," Gwen interjected. "I'm having trouble believing that."

"You can ask Boris about it when we rescue him, but I can assure you we have no reason to lie to you," Eradore said.

"I don't think you're lying. I just think you're mistaken," Gwen replied.

"There is a way to find out for certain," Aimil said.

That caught Gwen's attention. "How?"

"There's a place in the kingdom of Steepcross that can reveal a mage's true name. It's southeast of here, but if you want to know bad enough, the journey is worth it."

"I'll keep that in mind. Tell me about the rune you can show me."

"You're an eager one, aren't you?" Aimil asked, cracking a smile.

"I want to rescue my father, but Eradore won't let me leave until I've learned a rune."

"Eradore is wise, and I agree with him on this. There are many runes that you can learn, but the first one is the hardest and most painful."

"Painful?" Gwen asked.

"Yes. Once you learn the rune, it is burned into your flesh. The first rune has crippled many mages, but it's temporary. Even if it doesn't incapacitate you, it *will* hurt."

Gwen could feel her anxiety rising again, but

she kept the thought of her father in the forefront of her mind and it kept her from giving in. "Is every mage's first rune the same?"

"No," Aimil answered. "Every mage can choose their first rune, to an extent."

"What do you mean?" Gwen asked.

"Well, most runes you learn will come from another mage teaching it to you. As you can see," Aimil lifted her arms for emphasis, "I have learned many. You can choose from my runes which one you want to learn."

"What if I want to learn more than one?"

"You can't. A mage can only give one run to another mage."

"Why?" Gwen asked.

"No one is really sure," Aimil replied. "It's been a mystery for as long as there has been magic."

"So to get more runes, I have to find other mages to teach me?"

"Yes, but I would offer a word of caution. Not all mages are willing to share their secrets, so you will encounter mages who will refuse your request. They are few, though. Mages tend to favor academia, so most are open to teaching others."

"What kind of runes do you have?" Gwen leaned closer, looking over the numerous brands. There was one that caught her attention. It was shaped like a flower surrounded by a circle. "What is that one?"

"I want to try something," Aimil said. "Instead of telling you what my runes do, I want you to look at each one and tell me which you are most drawn to. Before we do that, though, I want to eat something. I'm famished!"

Gwen had completely forgotten about food in the midst of her curiosity. She had to force herself to be patient as they ate a small meal composed of eggs and roasted potatoes. Eradore and Aimil chatted about various things that Gwen found dull compared to magic. She cut a piece of bread from a fresh loaf and chewed on it as she agonized over how slow time was passing.

She had zoned out as she pondered who her real parents might be, assuming what Tobias and Eradore had said was true. Perhaps she came from a family of Prestiges? That would explain her magical inclination. Yet, why would they have abandoned her? Maybe she was born to a family that had an aversion to magic and feared having a Prestige as a daughter? Gwen was so deep in thought she hadn't noticed Aimil was looking at her.

"I'm sorry?"

"I asked if you were ready to pick a rune," Aimil replied.

"Yes, I'm ready."

Aimil laid her arms out onto the table. "Look at each one. Take in the details and point to the ones that stand out to you."

At first, Gwen thought the task would be easy. Yet as she studied the runes, it became apparent that it would take some time to see them all. Once she'd viewed all of the runes on Aimil's arms, the women stood and removed her upper armor, exposing her nakedness. Gwen's cheeks flushed with embarrassment, but Eradore's expression remained impassive.

"Keep going," Aimil said.

Gwen hesitantly continued perusing the runes. Aimil had more than Gwen could keep count of, and she wondered how long it had taken the woman to learn them all. The scarred brands continued from her arms and across her chest. Gwen made a pained look when she saw they were even on Aimil's breasts. Her stomach was smooth unmarred flesh, but the runes wound around to her back. There was one that looked like a wing that caught her attention. Gwen touched it softly.

"The Wing," Aimil said.

"How did you know which one I touched?" Gwen asked.

"I know my body," she said. It was all she offered as an explanation.

Gwen continued and touched one that looked like two cresting waves of water. She touched another that resembled what she thought was a fish, and the last one looked like a serpent, though its body was a zig-zag. Aimil removed her pants, leaving her intimate area covered only by a loincloth. Again, Gwen blushed, but she knelt and examined the runes on Aimil's legs. There were none that drew her eye, and she stood.

"Is that all of them? Gwen asked.

"There is one more, but you don't need to see it. Its only purpose is for pleasure."

Gwen thought for sure that her cheeks couldn't get any hotter, but they burned more fiercely at Aimil's words.

"You've chosen four," Eradore said. "Yet you can only have one."

"Which one pulls at you the most?" Aimil asked.

Gwen looked at the ones she had picked again, and she was most drawn to the undulated snake. "This one," she said, touching it. "The snake."

"Interesting," Aimil said.

"What?" Gwen asked.

"Nothing. It's a good choice. That's a powerful rune, though. You're definitely going to feel this one."

That caused Gwen some concern, but she had quickly come to realize from their conversation that power would come at a cost. "So how does this work? What do I need to do?"

"We need to go somewhere … higher," Aimil said, looking at Eradore.

The elf smiled knowingly and rose from his chair. "Follow me."

He led them to a stairway that only went upward, and they eventually reached the ceiling. A rectangular metal door rested in the center, surrounded by stones. Eradore pushed the door up, and they stepped out onto the roof of the tower. Gwen looked around, confused. Other than the tower, she could see nothing but thick gray fog.

"What is that?" she asked.

"It is the Ether," Eradore answered. "Remember, the top of this tower exists outside of the natural world."

"It's basically a pocket of space carved out magically, much like a cave," Aimil said. "Wizard stuff."

Gwen nodded, but it didn't make any sense to

her. She walked to the edge of the roof and looked down. The city of Penshaw was nothing more than a speck far below. Gwen backed away, afraid she might slip and fall to her death.

"You're going to need some protection," Aimil told Eradore. He closed his eyes and muttered something. A sphere of shifting green energy surrounded him.

"I want you to close your eyes," Aimil said. "Clear your mind of everything. It might be difficult, but you must have no distractions."

Gwen did as Aimil asked and closed her eyes, but she was having trouble purging her thoughts. It took a long while, but neither Eradore nor Aimil rushed her. When her mind was clear, she saw the zig-zag snake rune floating in the darkness, similar to her experience with the *bunús* rune.

Speak it, a voice whispered in her mind. She recognized it as Aimil's. It sounded like an echo, and it repeated several times before fading. Gwen focused intently on the rune but it was fuzzy and the name evaded her. She envisioned her hand and reached for it. Intense heat assaulted her and she jerked away.

You can do it, Aimil's voice echoed.

Gwen clenched her jaw and reached again. She ignored the heat and this time managed to grasp the rune. She pulled it closer until the fuzziness became clear and the name of the rune hit her like a blow.

"*Tintreach,*" Gwen uttered aloud.

Searing light suddenly filled the darkness. Gwen opened her eyes, but the light was still there, blinding her, burning her. She screamed, but if any sound came out, she didn't hear it. Her heartbeat slowed, but each beat was excruciatingly loud. She'd gone blind, and deafness followed. Gwen had a feeling of weightlessness, like gravity no longer existed for her. The light faded, and as her vision cleared, she realized why she felt so light.

She'd fallen off the tower.

CHAPTER 14

Conal

"OK, suppose I accept that I'm the long-lost son of some dead king –"

"He was your father," Bryok gently scolded. "You should show some respect."

"Why?" Conal challenged. "I never knew him. I feel nothing for him."

"You don't know him because he sent you away to protect you."

"From whom?"

"Torian."

"Torian? The guy who wants me dead? How old is this guy?"

"Not as old as you'd think," Bryok cryptically answered. "Perhaps I'd better explain. Would you like something to drink?"

"Is this a long story?"

"I'll make it brief," Bryok replied, taking an iron poker by the fireplace and jabbing at the embers. "Your father, King Kamron, ruled the kingdom of Isentol. He had two children."

"That's right," Conal interrupted. "I supposedly have a sister. Where's she?"

"I don't know. She was not my concern."

"So there are others like you looking for her?"

Bryok turned to appraise the young man, brash yet quite intelligent. "Not only those like me, remember. Torian too has his henchmen looking for her."

Conal tilted his head in thought. "If he sent me as far west as possible, logically he would have sent my sister in the opposite direction, as far east as possible."

"A logical assumption," Bryok acknowledged with a nod, "though he might have thought his enemies would think the same thing."

"Good point. Forget it. You were saying?"

"Kamron sent his children to safety to be raised by noble-hearted parents, people whose trust and faithfulness were beyond question."

Conal bolted to standing. "My God, anyone who thinks I'm Kamron's son knows where my parents are. We need to go back. We gotta save them."

Bryok turned solemn. "It is too late to go back."

Conal's eyes hardened and his jaw clenched. "They're…"

"Dead."

Conal blinked tears away. "When?"

"Almost a year ago."

Conal sucked in a breath. "A year ago?" Guilt washed through him. Here he was complaining about Kamron when he was less than a dutiful son. He had justified his absence as necessary in order to accumulate wealth. He was going to surprise them, return the wealthy son and set up shop with his father. His parents would be proud. But wealth was elusive, and he had drifted farther away.

"There was nothing you could have done," Bryok soothed. "They knew the risk involved."

Conal's heart thumped, afraid of the answer to his next question. "What about my brother and sisters?"

Bryok shook his head.

Conal clenched his fists and snarled, "Someone is going to pay for this. Wait a minute. You said this happened a year ago. Why would you even know about it?"

"I was alerted when Torian's assassins descended on Urve. Not long after their arrival, a jeweler and his family were caught in a fire. Coincidence? Hardly. Though assassins are good, they are still human. I have a friend in Urve who stumbled on the assassins in the act. He was lucky to escape alive. It caused me to wonder why Torian would send his fiends so far? I've been waiting and watching ever since. Now that you are here, a piece of the puzzle has been solved… a very big piece."

Conal inhaled an angry breath. "Like I said, someone is going to pay for this."

"And so they should," Bryok agreed. "But we can't go off without a plan."

Conal folded his arms and stared into the fire. "My destiny is to reclaim my father's kingdom?"

"Yes."

"How can I do that? I have no army, no followers, and no resources. It's not like I can just walk in and shout, 'Hey. I'm Kamron's son. Get off my throne.' And how am I going to convince anyone if I'm not convinced myself?"

"Things are already moving. It's just a question of fitting in and adapting them to your needs. Still, there are a few things you need to know."

"Like what?" Conal crossed back to his chair and sat, slouching back, his arms folded. His anger still smoldering, his mind raced with the methods of pain he would inflict on those responsible for his family's deaths. He knew he should feel intense sadness, but the only emotion that swirled within him was vengeance.

"Well, for starters, Torian just happens to be your uncle." Bryok placed the poker in the stand and pulled the chair out farther from the desk and sat.

Conal's head flopped back as he stared at the granite ceiling. "Why does that not surprise me? What you're telling me my uncle killed both my real father and my other father and family."

"Yes."

"Why?"

"You know the old saying, 'The more power a man has, the more he wants. The more he wants, the more he will do to get it.' You uncle was not satisfied to be number two. And then there is Grimmar the Mage-Breaker. It seems that all the trouble started when Grimmar came to Torian's court."

"Back to my original question," Conal said. "How am I supposed to overthrow a king when I have no assets or resources?"

"We get them along the way," Bryok smiled, "starting in Gurim-duhr."

"The dwarf kingdom? I thought you said the dwarf king was under Grimmar's spell."

"He is. We must break the chain that binds him to Grimmar."

"How do we do that?"

"We must remove Grimmar's man, Havyrd Twin-Tongue."

"Twin-tongue?"

"Remember what I said. Havyrd is not one to be trifled with. He is called 'Twin-Tongue' because he has the power of words and voice. In one instant he'll convince you to follow him and in the next instant hand you a knife and tell you to kill yourself to prove your devotion… and you would do it. To defeat him, he must not be allowed to speak. Once anyone hears his voice, they are condemned to follow his words."

"By the gods," Conal marveled. "Had I that gift I'd be a rich man by now." *And maybe my family would still be alive…*

"Wanting wealth is oft times like wanting power," Bryok quietly reminded him. "The more one gets, the more one wants."

"Sort of moot at the moment," Conal grimly chuckled. "So where do we start? I mean, what's the plan? How do we get to this Havyrd guy without getting trapped?"

"Very carefully."

Conal shook his head in irritation. "I'm serious. Right now there's you and me. Not overwhelming odds."

"Help is on the way. In fact, he should be here any moment."

"He? That's it? One more person?" His retort was interrupted by the sound of the hidden door scraping open, causing him to jerk upright and swivel around in time to see Drustan and Rhonyn enter.

Conal leaped up, his eyes darting to Bryok whose welcoming smile to the visitors told him he had been betrayed.

"I was hoping he was with you," Drustan smiled back. Seeing the panic in Conal's eyes, he soothed, "Perhaps I was hasty, my young friend."

"I'm not your friend," Conal shot back then turned to Bryok. "You bastard."

"It's not what you think," Bryok placated.

"You don't know what I think."

"Maybe if you shut up and listen," Rhonyn snipped, "you'd learn the truth."

At that moment two dwarves stepped into the room, the door closing behind them. "How about something to drink?" Torgreth grinned. "A nice cold ale would do."

Conal's mouth gaped wide. "Torgreth? Voldar?"

"At your service," Voldar replied with a sweeping bow.

Conal's brow bent in a deep furrow as his head twitched and his gaze flickered from one person to another. When none of them made any threatening gestures, he jammed his arms on his hips. "Will someone please explain what's going on?"

"That's better," Rhonyn said. "I'll let the two druids explain. I could use an ale." Without waiting for a reply, he headed for the door, turning to the dwarves. "You coming?"

"Wouldn't miss a cold brew," Voldar readily agreed, catching up, Torgreth on his heels.

Once Rhonyn and the two dwarves left the room, Drustan narrowed his gaze at Conal. "You're a hard man to keep up with." When Conal didn't reply, he said, "Perhaps I was hasty in my initial assessment. Why did you run?"

"You wanted to kill me," Conal retorted.

"I never said that," he lied

"Maybe not to me." Conal gave him a look that said he knew the man's intent.

Drustan warily studied the young man. How could he have known what was said to Rhonyn? "Like I said, I may have been hasty."

"So you admit you wanted me dead." Conal curled a lip. "Suppose you had succeeded?"

"I was wrong," Drustan huffed. "Can we move on. You're not dead. What's done is done."

"Is that some sort of an apology? 'Gee. So sorry I meant to kill you. Nothing personal you understand. Just business.'" Conal flopped back in his chair, crossing a leg over the other.

"Yes it was just business," Drustan answered, a smile curling the corners of his lips. "I made a snap decision that you might be in the way. I was wrong. Fortunately you were faster than I expected. After I explained my purpose to Voldar and Torgreth they agreed to return with me to find you. Luckily Bryok was here to keep you safe."

Conal's look said he wasn't convinced. "So… do you think I'm the long-lost son of King what's-his-name?"

"He's your father," Bryok reprimanded, "and he has a name. Use it."

"OK, OK, King Kamron."

"Apparently I'm not the only one unconvinced," Drustan taunted.

"Look at it from my point of view," Conal said, rolling his eyes. "Going from highwayman to king's son is quite a stretch."

Drustan turned to Bryok. "Have you found anything?"

"I was about to try the naming bone when you arrived."

"What's that?" Conal asked.

"A name is an essence," Bryok explained. "When parents give a child a name, it connects who they are with what they intend their child's future to be. It is a future and a history at the same time."

"And the bone?"

"It will show us if you are who we believe you to be."

"Will it hurt?" Conal groused, remembering the two instances of pain.

"Not in the same way," Bryok answered. "It is not a physical pain."

"Sometimes there is no pain at all," Drustan added. "It all depends on the parents and child. The links are strongest between father and son or mother and daughter. Though rare, links can cross. When that happens, it means the dominant parent has implanted the child's future."

Conal exhaled an exasperated sigh. "All this is mumbo jumbo. The bottom line is what will the naming bond tell you?"

"It will tell us the truth of your connection," Bryok said.

"I assume I have a birth name?"

"Yes. Darrbie."

"Darrbie?" Conal blurted. "My father named me Darrbie? What kind of name is that?"

"It means 'one who is free from hatred and

envy.' You don't like it?" Bryok asked.

"I am *not* going to be called Darrbie," Conal exclaimed. "I don't care who my father is."

"That is your choice," Drustan said. "But for now, consent to use the name so we can establish heritage."

"Darrbie," Conal sneered. "Sounds like a girl's name." Looking at them, he asked, "What's my sister's name?"

"Her real name or the name she is using?" Bryok replied.

"Both."

"We don't know what name she uses. Her birthname is Quinlee. It means 'woman of wisdom and insight.'"

Conal curled a lip. "Our parents named us Darrbie and Quinlee? What is wrong with them? What kind of parent would name their kids Darrbie and Quinlee? This sounds like part of a joke."

"Can we proceed?" Drustan interrupted. "You can rant and rage later."

"Yeah, sure… but Darrbie? I mean, c'mon. Free from envy and hatred? Talk about way off the mark. First thing I'm gonna do when I find Oscon is torture the living stuffing out of him then kill him. How's that for being free of hatred?"

"Shall we begin?" Bryok said, ignoring him. Pulling out the bottom right drawer of the desk, he lifted out something wrapped in cloth. Placing it on the desktop, he unwrapped it, displaying an animal bone with runes carved into it.

"This is a naming bone," he explained. "It will give us the answers we seek."

"What animal?" Conal asked.

"It is from the femur of a stag."

"Is a stag required?"

"Yes. Now quit interrupting." He handed the bone to Conal. "All you need to do is hold the bone with both hands and say, 'I am Darrbie.' The bone will do the rest."

"That's it?" Conal regarded the bone in his hands. It was smooth, sliced clean at both ends. Engraved in black letters were runes and symbols he didn't recognize or understand. Inhaling a deep breath, he placed his feet shoulder-width apart and grasped the bone with both hands. "Might as well get this over with… I am Darrbie."

The bone grew warmer and a faint orange glow surrounded the bone and his hands. Suddenly he was filled with overwhelming grief, like watching someone he loved executed before his eyes. His eyes slammed shut as the vision consumed him. Blood pooled beneath the body of a man on the ground, his purple robe stained. The jeweled crown that once adorned his head lay close by. Beside him, a lovely woman wearing a golden crown slumped to her knees, the hilt of a dagger protruding from her chest.

He cried out as she slumped to the ground. His hand involuntarily shot out as though trying to catch her. Her head slowly turned, and her eyes found his. With her last breaths, she smiled and mouthed the words, 'My son.'

Conal cried out and flung the bone from his hands. Opening his eyes, he felt hot and wiped away the sweat from his forehead and face. His hands felt even hotter and he looked down to see runes slowly fading from his palms.

Shifting a look between Drustan and Bryok whose satisfied grin told him they were pleased with the results, he said, "Well?"

"What did you see?"

Conal related the vision and the pain he felt.

"You didn't see it because your eyes were closed," Bryok commented, "but the color surrounding your hands turned from orange to pure white, which means you are truly Kamron's son."

Stunned, Conal remained rooted to the floor, trying to make sense of everything. He had hoped it was all a mistake, that he could go back to the way things were before. But then he remembered that nothing was the same anymore. His family was dead… and he was now a king's son.

"I need a drink."

"That can be arranged," Bryok chuckled.

"By the way," Drustan casually said. "What do you know about dragons?"

CHAPTER 15

Gwen

Gwen's eyes widened in terror as she fell.

She kicked her legs and flapped her arms as if that would help, and suddenly her descent ended, harsh and abrupt. Had she really just stopped her fall by flailing her limbs about? She flapped her arms again, and this time she rose through the air. Her body continued rising until she topped the tower, where she hovered for a moment before landing gently on the roof.

"How did I do that?" she exclaimed excitedly.

"You didn't," Aimil said, nodding to Eradore. "He did."

Eradore frowned. "I didn't expect the lightning to fling you off the tower. There will be better precautions in the future."

When Gwen realized it wasn't the ridiculous arm flapping that had stopped her fall, she laughed. She was thankful nobody had seen her lame impression of a bird.

"I thought that rune was a snake."

"No, it's a lightning bolt," Aimil replied. "Now that you say that, I can see some similarity. Do you feel any pain?"

"A little."

Gwen lifted her left hand, cupping it with her right one. On the back of her hand, where the lightning bolt rune had been seared, the skin was swollen and bright red. Her flesh throbbed, but otherwise she felt like her usual self.

"She's strong," Aimil said to Eradore. "The last mage who took that rune couldn't walk or see for two days."

"How do I use the rune?" Gwen asked.

"She's also impatient," Eradore said. "I'm going to leave her with you for a while. I have some things to attend to that I've been putting off."

"She's in good hands," Aimil said. "Mind if I join the attack on the outpost? I'd love to strike at King Torian's soldiers."

"I'm sure Tobias and Roland would love to have you along. They're finalizing a few things, and they should be here within the hour." Eradore turned to Gwen. "I hope to see you again before I leave, but if I don't, please return here after the outpost is dealt with."

Gwen hadn't thought past the attack on the outpost, and she found herself suddenly reeling mentally. What would come after they rescued her father? He couldn't go back to the Seven Stars. If it was still standing, it belonged to the king. What would they do? *One thing at a time,* Gwen reminded herself.

"I will," she promised Eradore.

Eradore went back into the tower and Gwen looked at Aimil. The image of her nakedness was burned into Gwen's mind, and it was hard for her to look at the woman without feeling embarrassed.

"What?" Aimil asked.

"Nothing," Gwen replied quickly.

"Spit it out. There's no need for secrets."

"The runes on your ... uh ..." Gwen motioned

to her chest.

"Yes?"

"What do they do? And why are they there?"

Aimil shrugged. "The magic puts the runes where it deems best. I've never questioned that. As to what they do?" Aimil looked around. "I suppose this is the best place to show you."

Gwen watched as Aimil lifted her right hand, arm extended. She tilted her hand back so that her palm was facing away from her and said, "*Guairneán.*"

The gray clouds where Aimil motioned began to swirl. It started slowly but quickly increased until there was a powerful whirlwind spinning among the clouds. The wind whistled loudly, and Gwen's shirt lashed about. The force continued to grow until Gwen felt her footing start to slip. She grabbed onto Aimil for support.

Aimil looked at her. The woman's eyes held a wild look, like an enraged animal Gwen had seen once. It scared her and she released Aimil, more willing to be pulled into the whirlwind than to see what insanity Aimil might unleash, but the whirlwind slowed and faded altogether.

"The magic is addictive," Aimil said after the silence grew awkward.

"How so?"

"Have you ever been drunk?" Aimil turned around and Gwen saw the crazy look in the woman's eyes was gone.

"Yes," Gwen replied.

"After you've had a few tankards, you feel good, loosened up. And as the feeling grows, you like it and want more, so you drink more, yes?"

Gwen nodded.

"It's like that, only much more primal. Controlling the magic once a rune is activated can be hard. If you aren't careful, you can destroy everything around you. When you use the magic, it must be for a purpose. Wielding it at random will make you a danger to yourself and those around you."

"I understand," Gwen said. "I've never wanted to hurt anyone, even when I was angry. That won't change."

"It might," Aimil warned. "Power changes people."

Gwen decided not to argue with her. "How do I make the rune work like you did?"

"Do you feel the pulsing in your skin, where the rune is?"

"The pain?" Gwen asked.

"No. Search beyond the pain. You'll know the difference when you feel it."

Gwen looked at the rune on her own hand and mentally navigated past the stinging pain. Something pulsed softly. When she touched it with her mind, it zapped her, making her eyes water.

"You found it," Aimil said, stifling her mirth. "When you are ready to use it, you will focus on that pulse and speak the name of the rune. The magic will channel through you. Remember! Control is important. If you lose control, you may not live through the experience."

"I have a question," Gwen said.

"Ask."

"When I came through Eradore's mirror portal, my body was fighting the magic. It's a bit confusing, but I felt something inside me align with my spine. The *bunús*. What is it?"

"The *bunús* is like the cornerstone of a building, the base that all runes are built upon. It enables a mage to become a vessel for the magic."

"Can a mage lose the ability to use runes? And do runes lose their strength?" Gwen asked.

"If a mage isn't in control of their mind, such as being drunk, the magic will be weaker. I've never heard of anyone completely losing the magic. Runes are as powerful or as weak as you allow. There are limits to magic, of course, but they are … high ceilings."

"You said power changes people. Did it change you?"

"Without a doubt," Aimil answered. "Believe it or not, I was once very meek. People pushed me around and I let them. Once I became a mage, I sought out every rune I could find. As I gained them and became stronger, I stopped allowing people to take advantage of me."

Gwen's eyes widened. "You were meek? You seem so …"

"Loud? Brash?"

"No," Gwen said. "Powerful."

Aimil laughed. "Maybe a little. Sometimes too much."

"What do you mean?"

Aimil grew serious. "I was married to a soldier. He would abuse me physically. Hit me, things like that. One day I decided it was enough. I'd gained only a handful of runes then, but they were sufficient."

"Sufficient for what?" Gwen asked.

"Sufficient to kill him. I called fire and burned him until he stopped screaming."

Gwen decided it was a good idea to never anger Aimil. "That's … I'm sorry you had to endure his abuse."

"I'm sure he was, too, in the end. Let's forget about this. Remembering the past causes me to feel things I'd rather not."

"How did you meet Eradore?" Gwen asked, changing the subject.

"Ah, now that's a story. A host of goblins had somehow gotten into the city and began burning and ransacking. I was the first to show up and Eradore joined me. We put down the goblins together and ended up becoming friends."

"Is that how you got involved with the rebellion, too? Knowing Eradore?"

"I'm actually the one who convinced him to aid us. He wanted to remain neutral, but as Torian's soldiers continued to cause suffering, he changed his mind. His passion for the people is hard to rival. You'd think that since he's an elf he wouldn't care about humans, but that couldn't be further from the truth."

Gwen's respect for Eradore continued to increase the more she learned about him. Her hand still throbbed, and she traced the rune with her finger, careful not to touch the inflamed skin.

"When will the pain go away?" she asked.

"Considering how well you took the rune, I'd

guess a day or so. I'm impressed you're even coherent, let alone conscious. Like I told Eradore, the last person I know who took the lightning rune was out for two days. You're made of tough stuff."

"I don't think so," Gwen said.

Aimil closed her eyes and muttered something under her breath, then looked at Gwen. "Tobias and Roland are here."

"How do you know?"

"Eradore told me." Aimil pointed to a rune on her left arm. It looked like two skulls with a thin string between them. "Let's get back inside. I'm sure you two have some catching up to do."

Gwen followed Aimil back into the tower and closed the metal door behind her. They found Tobias and Roland at the terrace and Gwen felt a flood of emotion when she saw Tobias. The night her father had been captured hadn't been long ago, yet it felt to her like weeks had passed. She wrapped Tobias in a hug.

"Everything all right?" he asked, awkwardly returning her embrace.

"Yes, I'm just glad you're back."

"Right. Well, everything is in place. Have you seen Eradore? I was going to let him know that the soldiers who followed us here have been snooping around, trying to get information on our whereabouts."

"He said he had to take care of some things," Gwen replied. "I find it odd they haven't gone back to the outpost."

"I'm sure it has something to do with you," Tobias said. "I don't think they chased us over that horse."

"Why would they have been chasing me?"

"Who knows? How's the time with Eradore been? Did you learn any—" He paused when he saw the rune on her hand. "So, you *are* a mage. I did not see that coming."

"Neither did I," Gwen said. "I wasn't sure about all of this. The rebellion, my father, magic … all of it, but now I think it was all meant to happen the way it did for a reason."

"Only time will tell," Tobias smiled at her. "You seem different somehow."

"What do you mean?"

"It's hard to put into words, but it's not a bad thing. It's just different."

Gwen gave him an odd look and shrugged. "When are we leaving? Eradore said my father wasn't doing well, and I want to get there as quickly as we can. It's already been too long for my comfort."

"Roland has organized everything, so we can leave now. I wanted to speak to Eradore, but I can talk to him when we get back. I found out an interesting bit of information while I was out."

"Oh? What is it?"

"I can't say. Not yet, anyway."

"Then why did you bring it up to begin with? Now I'm curious," Gwen huffed.

"Let's get going," Tobias said, ignoring her comment. "I want to get there before nightfall."

They left Eradore's tower and wound their way down the maze of streets, ending at the main gates leading out of the city. As they walked, Gwen studied Roland. He was taller than her by a full foot and had black hair that was cut so short she questioned the purpose of even keeping it. A jagged scar ran the length of his right cheek. Roland walked with a confident bearing that showed he was a leader. A sword was sheathed at his side, the leather that covered the hilt well-worn from use.

Gwen looked from him to Tobias and could understand why Tobias didn't want to lead the attack. With someone like Roland at the head, people were probably more likely to willingly join the danger. Even then, attacking an outpost filled with trained soldiers sounded insane. And yet here she was, walking toward danger herself to rescue her father. Eradore had told her that she could ask Boris the truth about her relation to him. What if he corroborated what Tobias and Eradore said?

Again, Gwen found herself occupied with things she didn't need to focus on. They left the city behind and soon joined a small camp of men and women. Most of them were human, but Gwen spotted a few elves among their numbers.

"We're going to ride quick, but I don't want anyone pushing their animals too hard," Roland announced once everyone had gathered around him. "You were all told to keep your lips sealed about this little foray, and I hope you've all kept your word. Keep your eyes open, regardless. We don't want any surprises in case there are rats among us. Any questions?" Roland paused and glanced around. "Head out!"

There weren't enough horses for everyone to ride alone, so Gwen chose to ride with Tobias. The group of horses trotted along at a decent pace, but Gwen remembered their harrowing ride to Penshaw and found their speed to be much slower.

"So, what's this interesting bit of information you want to share with Eradore?" Gwen asked.

"You're going to keep asking until I say, aren't you?"

"Probably," Gwen said. "Probably meaning yes."

Tobias turned to look over his shoulder at her. She smiled at him, but his expression was troubled. "Listen," he lowered his voice. "I don't know if it's true, but the soldiers who followed us aren't from the outpost."

"They aren't? But that's the direction they came from."

"I know." Tobias glanced around to make sure no one had taken an interest in their conversation. "We already guessed they were using magic to track us, but we didn't know why. I think I know why now."

"Why?"

"They're looking for the daughter of the king."

"Torian has a daughter?" Gwen asked.

"Not Torian," Tobias clarified. "Kamron. There's always been rumors that his children escaped the slaughter, but the heat is picking up on those stories now. People are saying that Torian knows they survived and he's looking for them."

"What does any of that have to do with us?"

"Not us, Gwen. You."

"Me? What are you talking about?"

"I think you're Kamron's missing daughter."

CHAPTER 16

Conal

"Dragons?" Conal's face scrunched into a frown. "Where did that come from?"

"Just thinking of possibilities," Drustan said.

"Why don't you just wish for pixie dust and magical unicorns while you're at it?" Conal taunted. "Have you ever seen a dragon?"

"Yes, I have."

Conal fixed him with a sharp eye, waiting for the punchline. "You're serious."

"Yes," Drustan replied, "though it's been a while."

"A real dragon?"

"Yes." Drustan repeated. "Believe it or not, there was a time when dragons were rather common."

"Until the Hunting," Bryok sourly added.

"The Hunting?"

"That's what it was called," Bryok explained. "One hundred and fifty years ago, when Odhran was king in Tul Cragbyrn, he declared dragons an enemy to all the races."

"Why?" Conal asked, his thirst momentarily forgotten.

"Gold," Drustan answered, "and silver and other precious things."

"Dragons had accumulated a vast amount of wealth," Bryok continued, "and Odhran wanted it. Isentol was once the dragon kingdom and

Havengarde was the citadel, a sacred place for dragons."

"Why?"

"Does it matter why?" Bryok said. "That it was sacred to them is sufficient enough. Dwarves have their sacred mountains, humans their sacred burial grounds and elves… well who knows about elves." His smile quickly vanished. "It became open season on dragons. Celebrations erupted with each killed dragon."

"As you can imagine," Drustan said, "after a while it got harder and harder to find dragons. Finally, dragons disappeared."

"Yet you've seen one." Conal's scoffed.

"Yes. Why do you persist in unbelief?"

"Because no one even talks about them anymore." Conal folded his arms. "Other than your supposed sighting, dragons might as well be nonexistent. Why bring them up now?"

Drustan shifted a glance at Bryok. "I raise the issue because dragons do exist and it would be to your advantage to enlist their help."

Conal stared at him a moment before shaking his head. "First you tell me that I'm some dead king's son. Then you want me to get rid of some guy who can talk me into killing myself, but along the way, we're gonna look for dragons. Is that about right?"

"Pretty much," Bryok smiled. "Yet you fail to ask the important question, which is, 'Why are we so confident that we can find a dragon?'"

"OK… I'll bite. Why are you so confident?"

Bryok smiled. "Because we know where one

is."

The door opened and Rhonyn breezed in, the two dwarves on his heels, each carrying two steins of ale.

"My compliments on the ale, Master Bryok," Torgreth commented, handing a stein to Conal. "Some of the best we've had in a while."

Conal hooked a thumb at Drustan. "I thought you two were on the run from him."

"We thought so too. Knew Rorkyn was lookin' for us and figured he sent him after us."

"Wasn't until he explained what was goin' on that we realized we were running from the wrong guy," Voldar added. "You were already down river by then. Nice reaction time by the way." He grinned and turned to Bryok. "No sooner had the door opened that he was out the window. Never seen anyone move so fast."

"Survival instinct," Conal shrugged then turned an accusing glare at Drustan. "If you knew then you were wrong, why all the arrows at me when I dove in?"

"Accidental," Rhonyn answered. "Had a few archers react before I could stop them."

Voldar took a draught of ale before asking Bryok, "So? Is he the one?"

"Yes."

Voldar slapped his thigh. "Excellent. Then we got us a chance."

"When do we start?" Torgreth enthused.

"Whoa, not so fast," Conal interrupted. "What's the plan?"

"Eliminate Havyrd," Voldar stated. "He's the

cause of our problems."

"How?" Rhonyn inserted himself into the discussion. "We've been over this ground before. Yeah, we have the king's son. So what? He's as human as the rest of us."

"Hey," Torgreth complained.

"I mean he's as susceptible to Havyrd's tongue as the rest of us are. How are we going to get to Havyrd without compromising ourselves? We've got to cross into Gurim-duhr then get into Morendir without anyone noticing us. Considering we've got two druids with us as well as the two dwarves he's been searching for, not to mention the 50 plus folks of my team, we're going to be easy to spot." He turned his attention to the two dwarves. "What did you two do that has Havyrd chasing you?"

"We got nervous making more rune bones and dice," Voldar answered, "and seeing more of our kin enslaved to Havyrd's foul desires." He shook his head in disgust. "It's bad enough Rorkyn is under his spell. What's worse is that Twin-Tongue isn't even a dwarf."

"He's not?" Conal sputtered, surprised.

"No. He's human, a mealy excuse of a man. If not for the power of his tongue, he'd be the kind you'd kick out of your way."

"This doesn't get us anywhere," Rhonyn complained. "We still have to get into Morendir undetected."

"I have an idea," Conal quietly announced. "We split up and meet inside the city somewhere."

"All of us?" Rhonyn raised an eyebrow in objection.

"No. You and your team head across the northern part of Gurim-duhr like you're heading towards Clagmoran. Word will get out and their attention will be diverted to you while the rest of us head south to Morendir."

"Then what?" Voldar cocked an eyebrow. "It's not like they won't be looking for my brother and me."

"And it's not like traveling with two druids will go unnoticed," Torgreth chimed in.

"We disguise ourselves and split up, one dwarf with one druid. No one's looking for me, so I'll be the third wheel with one group."

"Disguise ourselves as what?" Voldar asked, not much impressed with the idea, nor walking back into the proverbial hornet's nest in Morendir.

"Merchants or something," Conal huffed. "I don't care, just something so that no one recognizes you."

"OK," Torgreth mused aloud. "Let's say we make it into the city. What then?"

"We meet at some rendezvous place. Havyrd is human, right? That means he needs to eat and sleep. He probably has some sort of routine. He can't spend all his time next to the king. He's gotta pee sometime."

Torgreth frowned in thought. "Actually, he does have a peculiar habit of taking a walk around the king's palace right after lunch when most folks are getting back to work."

"That's right." Voldar's eyes brightened. "He does it every day. But we'd still have to get into the palace."

"I think we might be able to help," Bryok said, focusing on Drustan. "Rune bones." When Drustan hesitated, he narrowed his stare. "It's important."

"Fine," Drustan relented.

"Rune bones?" Conal repeated, gazing at the two druids.

"We have a collection of rune bones we've accumulated over the years," Bryok explained, "all imbued with magic. I think we have some we can use to help subdue Havyrd."

"Subdue? That begs the question," Conal pointed out. "Do you want him captured or dead?"

"Dead," both dwarves chimed in.

"Dead," Bryok repeated, Drustan nodding agreement.

"What do I do when… I mean *if* you are unsuccessful?" Rhonyn asked.

"Do what seems best to you," Conal replied, "but if this is our only option, we can't fail."

"Too easily said."

"You have a better plan?"

"Not at the moment." Rhonyn turned his attention to the two druids. "Let's say we get the dwarves to join the cause; there's still Clagmoran and the other kingdoms to deal with. What's your plan to get Kilmaryn to join?"

"Vanity," Drustan answered. "Look up the definition for vanity and you'll see a picture of Kilmaryn."

"Who's Kilmaryn? Conal interrupted.

"King of Clagmoran," Drustan said. "I've had dealings with him before. He's a good king, cares about this people. But his kingdom is all he cares about. He's fortified his kingdom and until someone breaches the walls, he won't budge."

"First things first," Conal reminded them. "Once we get Havyrd taken care of, we can worry about Kilmaryn."

"When do we leave?" Voldar piped up.

"What time is it?" Conal asked.

"Late afternoon," Bryok answered. "We leave at midnight. Gives us a chance to escape unnoticed."

"Gates will be closed," Torgreth pointed out.

Bryok smiled knowingly. "We have other ways to get out." He turned to Rhonyn. "You can leave whenever you're ready."

"We'll leave in the morning. I'd better go check on my team."

Rhonyn drained the rest of his drink and placed his stein on the desk when Conal suddenly remembered something Bryok had mentioned and turned to him. "What about what you said about the dra–"

"We can talk about that later," Bryok interrupted, speaking over him before addressing Rhonyn. "We'll send word to you in Merthyl-haven."

"Right. Good luck to you." Rhonyn nodded to the others, waiting for Drustan to guide him back out the way they came in.

While Drustan led Rhonyn through the maze, Bryok informed the two dwarves that, "There's plenty of food and ale in the kitchen and buttery. Help yourselves while Conal and I talk more about our plans."

"Sounds like yer tryin' to get rid of us,"

Torgreth grinned.

"I am," he laughed. "Conal and I have some other personal matters to discuss."

"No need to ask twice," Torgreth said, "especially when there's food and ale. C'mon brother. Let's see what's in the larder."

Waiting until they were through the door, Bryok motioned for Conal to sit. "You need to be cautious when you talk about dragons. First, not everyone is willing to accept the truth and second, not everyone can be trusted. And third, is that there are still those who believe the only good dragon is a dead dragon. So from now on, let's just keep this between us."

"OK by me. You said you know where one is,"

"We do, but we have to be exceedingly cautious. Remember what we said about the Hunting?"

The epiphany hit and Conal abruptly realized his mistake. "You think the dwarves or Rhonyn's people would try to kill it."

"Not necessarily them, but if word got out…"

"I'll keep my mouth shut."

"Good," Bryok said. "Now there's one more thing we need to talk about. Your brand. What do you know about the Cobra assassin?"

"To be honest," Conal shrugged, "nothing other than they're supposed to be a leader among assassins."

"You are partially right." Bryok walked over to stand by the hearth, placing his fingers under the brim of the mantel. A door appeared in the stone wall. Retrieving a candelabra, he beckoned, "Come with me."

Conal followed him into a large room filled floor to tall ceiling with shelves containing small boxes, each box labeled with the contents in a script that he didn't recognize. Bryok paused in front of a shelf and pulled down a box, opening the lid.

"Rune bones?"

"All the boxes in here contain rune bones. It's taken us a while, but we've probably accumulated more incantation bones than anyone else is all the kingdoms."

"Even more than Grimmar?"

"Hopefully even more than him."

"We've intercepted a number of his shipments," Drustan interrupted, "which means he knows someone is trying to stop him."

"Which is why he was so intent on capturing the two dwarves," Bryok added.

Conal raised an eyebrow. "Why all the fuss? Why not simply have folks up wherever he is and have then carve runes right there?"

"Runes have to be carved exact," Bryok answered. "A misplaced serif on a letter or an incorrect angle of a line changes the rune and the spell with potential disastrous results. Dwarves are known for their expertise, Voldar and Torgreth being some of the best."

"So why not just kidnap them and bring them up there?"

"Too many problems with that," Dustan said.

Conal immediately understood. "They'd screwup a carving on purpose."

"Exactly."

Holding the box with one hand, Bryok picked a

small bone out, holding it between thumb and forefinger at the ends. "This box here contains bones marked with incantations for agility and speed." He held it up so Conal could see the runes.

"What does it say?"

Bryok smiled paternally at him. "It is a language you will learn later. For now, be content that it is for your good."

"What do I do with it?" He went to reach for it, but Bryok pulled back.

"Patience. Do you not want to know what happens when you receive a rune bone?"

Conal frowned, suddenly apprehensive. "Is this like the naming rune?"

"Not quite," he chuckled. "Every rune bone has a power imbued in it. In certain bones, once the power is transferred, the bone is nothing more than a mere bone, not even good for a dog to chew on. What happens when a bone user receives the power depends on the bone and the imbued power. But, what *will* happen is that the runes will be transferred to the user."

Conal glanced around the room at the number of boxes. "Have you used any of these?"

"Of course," he replied with a cryptic smile.

"Is it possible for one person to use all of them?"

"I suppose it's possible though it would not be prudent. Rune spells are not meant for everyone."

"Not everyone can use rune bones," Drustan pointed out, walking in. "Only individuals who are mage-marked can use rune bones. Anyone else who tries would suffer beyond description."

"And you think I'm mage-marked?" He cocked an eyebrow in doubt.

"Being mage-marked doesn't necessarily mean you are a mage," Bryok explained. "For some it means you are gifted with the ability to use rune bones to expand who you are."

Conal shifted his gaze around the room, noting the number of boxes and what must be thousands of rune bones. "Where did you find them all?"

"Various places. Here," he held the rune bone out to him. "Firmly grasp the bone so that the letters face your palm. The bone will get warm, maybe even hot. Whatever you do, do not let go of the bone until it cools."

Conal hesitated then took the bone in his right hand, rotating it so the runes faced his palm then griped it tightly.

At first, it felt nothing more than what it appeared, a bone with writing engraved on it. Then warmth radiated and he felt a tingling up his arm that radiated throughout his body. The bone grew warmer then hot, uncomfortably hot.

"Do not let go," Bryok warned then chanted a phrase that Conal did not understand.

The tingling turned into lightning charges and sweat dripped from his forehead.

"Keep holding it," Bryok encouraged.

Suddenly the burning and the pain stopped and whatever heat the bone had evaporated. Conal opened his hand and pulled the bone away, twirling it around only to discover the engraved writing had disappeared. He looked down at his hand and saw nothing. He looked up at Bryok who stood grinning at him like a proud father. "Where'd it go?"

"It has transferred to you. Check yourself."

It was when Conal checked his left forearm that he noticed it. The writing, in black runes the same size as on the bone, forever imprinted on his skin.

"What power do I now have?"

"Agility and speed. There are several other powers I suggest you take on."

"Like what?"

"Endurance and weapons. Speed is great, but if you grow tired after thirty seconds, what good it is to you?"

"Weapons?"

Bryok slowly nodded, inhaling a slow breath. "Just as there are more than one kind of weapon, there are more than one spell that will help. I suggest the normal sword and dagger but would also add throwing stars and nunchuks."

"Throwing stars? Nunchuks? What are they?"

"They are weapons every assassin needs."

Conal shook his head, furrowing his brows. "Just for the sake of argument, if I'm supposed to become king, why do I need to train to be an assassin?"

"How long will it take to become king? How many battles must you fight to claim the throne? What measures must you take to keep that throne?"

Conal blinked in understanding. "Point taken."

"You have natural leadership skills. You must now assume the role your brand has declared you. Do you wish to continue?"

Conal sucked in a deep breath, the heat and pain still a fresh memory. "Yeah. Might as well get this over with."

By the time Conal finished, seven sets of runes marked his body with the addition of strength and stealth runes. He was exhausted, glad it was over, yet intrigued with what other rune bones were there. Perhaps he would return and browse what was available... after he became king.

"Y'know," he said, still woozy from the spell transfers, and leaning against the door-jam, "What were those words you were saying when I held the bones?"

"Incantation words. In order for a rune to transfer, it needs to be unlocked. A rune can be unlocked one of two ways; either by the one holding the bone or a mage or wizard."

"Or a druid."

"Or a druid." He stared intently at him. "A word of caution. The incantation words must be pronounced correctly. Mispronounced words can result in some very unpleasant results... even death."

Conal eyes popped wide. "Point noted." His face morphed to a frown. "I always wondered why you're called a half-druid. What exactly does that mean?"

Bryok's smile faded. "It means what is says."

"I don't get it. Half of you is a druid. What's the other half?"

Bryok stood to full height. "It is something to be very afraid of. I have been placed into two worlds. Most of the time I live as a human, a druid, with the powers of a druid. The other world where I live is full of anger and hatred and resentment, spirit forces demanding to be unleashed. I have managed to keep them under control with the help of runes. I hope there will come a time when I can live in one world."

Conal noticed he didn't say which world. Glancing behind him, he noted that Drustan had gone to check on the dwarves. "What about Drustan? Is he like you?"

Bryok fixed him with a sharp stare. "Though he is my brother, be warned. The spirits have a greater hold on him. If he seems short tempered, it is because of the struggle of his worlds. I pray we can find an answer in time before he destroys us all."

CHAPTER 17

Gwen

The image of the slaughter from her vision came to the forefront of Gwen's mind.

"No," she said. "That's not possible."

"How do you know that for certain?" Tobias asked.

"Look at me. I'm nothing special. A princess would be …" Gwen shrugged. "Better? She'd be beautiful and … and, you'd just be able to tell. I don't know."

"You don't think you're beautiful?"

"Not really," Gwen replied.

"I do," Tobias said.

He turned his attention ahead, which Gwen was grateful for. Her cheeks were flushed, and she couldn't believe Tobias had complimented her like that. She did find him on the handsome side, but she had never looked at him in *that* way before. Yet as she thought about it now, it was possible that he was compatible with her.

Gwen debated with herself on what to say, but ultimately decided to keep her mouth shut. There were pressing issues, and a possible romance wasn't what she had in mind. At least, not yet.

The trip should have taken the better part of a single day, but as multiple problems arose, mainly with the horses, it took two days to reach the outskirts of the outpost. By the time the structure was within eyesight, they'd lost almost half their horses to a mysterious illness that caused the animals to weaken and collapse. Aimil had looked them over, but was unable to find what caused it.

All of the rebellion members were still accounted for, and most everyone was in high spirits despite the setbacks. There were a few grumblers, but they were quickly reminded of their mission by their fellows, and the complaints were silenced. Roland ordered them to set up camp and called a handful of men to his side, including Tobias. Gwen stayed out of the way and watched the others methodically erect tents and build a makeshift stable for the horses.

Gwen walked to the edge of the camp and stared at the stone structure, wondering where the soldiers were keeping her father. Eradore had said he wasn't doing well, but Gwen wasn't sure what that meant. Had he meant physically or mentally? Gwen berated herself for not asking questions.

"Hang in there," she whispered pleadingly. "We're coming for you."

It was midday and the sun hung overhead, the heat beating down mercilessly. There was no breeze to offer any respite, and the black clothing Gwen wore made her misery increase. Tobias eventually joined her, standing there like a silent guardian.

"What's the plan?" she asked.

"Roland wants to wait until night to begin the attack. He said the darkness will work in our favor and allow us to get close before we're spotted."

"Do you think they can see us from there? If we can see their walls, it seems likely they can see us."

"It's possible," Tobias admitted. "But they don't

know we're coming, so they shouldn't be on the lookout for anything out of the ordinary. And if they do spot us, they'll probably assume we're merchants."

Gwen hadn't considered that. Given the season, that seemed a logical assumption. Merchants frequently passed through Dawsbury this time of year, so it wouldn't be odd to see a group of them camped out beside the road. Still, something didn't feel right to Gwen.

"I'm scared," Gwen confessed.

"So am I," Tobias replied.

"Really?"

"Yes. It's one thing to talk about rebellion, and something entirely different to actually do it, be part of it. There's so much uncertainty."

Gwen was relieved to know she wasn't the only one feeling that way. She'd mistakenly assumed her father had been wrong to tell her to find Tobias, but little by little she'd come to see the wisdom of his request. Tobias was a good man and she was glad to have him at her side.

"When it gets dark, what are we doing?" Gwen asked.

"Roland is sending a few scouts ahead to make sure there are no surprises, then the rest of us will move in. The majority of us are going for the main building there." Tobias pointed to the largest part of the structure. "Smaller groups are going to hit the other two."

"Am I going with the largest group?"

"No," Tobias said hesitantly, quickly glancing at her from his periphery. "It's safer if you go with one of the smaller groups. They are less likely to encounter resistance. Once the main building has been secured, everyone else can join us there.”

Gwen wanted to argue with him, but her fear convinced her it was probably the better option. Once they'd taken the outpost, then she could safely free her father. She nodded mutely, ready for nightfall.

The time passed slower than Gwen cared for, despite the fact that she tried to keep herself busy. She helped with food preparation, used whetstones to sharpen the blades of swords, and batched loose arrows together for quivers. After she'd assisted with everything she could, it wasn't quite dusk yet. She spotted Aimil standing alone near one of the tents and walked over to her.

“I'm guessing you're going with the main group?” Gwen asked.

“I am. Roland said I'm too valuable of an asset not to. What about you?”

“No. I'm going with one of the smaller groups.”

“Is that what you want to do? I can convince Roland to let you come with us.”

“No, it's fine,” Gwen said. “I don't think I'm mean enough to fight my way into a fortress.”

Aimil snorted, but she had a smile on her face. “Wait until life spits on you enough. Then you'll get mean.”

“Other than your ex-husband, have you killed anyone?”

“Yes,” Aimil answered without hesitation. “The world can be a brutal place. I've found it's always better to strike first.”

Gwen thought that perspective was a bit harsh, but she didn't know everything Aimil had been through and didn't want to judge the woman.

"There are two things I value in this world," Aimil added. "Money and power. They rarely come one without the other."

"Why help with the rebellion, then? Eradore said their resources are limited compared to the king's."

"Some things are a mystery," Aimil replied, smiling again. "I'm going to rest until dark. I suggest you do the same."

Gwen was physically tired, but her mind was too alert to sleep. She watched Aimil disappear into the tent, then walked to her own and tried to sleep. Between the heat and her thoughts, it was impossible. She resigned herself to just lying there and let her mind wander until it was dark. The camp came alive with movement and she stepped out of her tent.

"Gwen!" It was Tobias. He motioned for her and she hurried to him. "You're going to be with Tylindra's group. She's taking the building on the far left."

A tall elven woman with golden brown hair tilted her head in acknowledgment. "Greetings, Gwen. I've given my word to Tobias that I'll make sure you are safe."

Gwen felt her face flush again and hoped the darkness hid her unspoken response. "Thank you," Gwen said. "I'll try not to get in the way."

"Once we've reached the main building, give us a few minutes before you attack. We want to make sure we've drawn most of the soldiers to us."

"As you command," Tylindra said.

Tobias left them and joined the larger group. They began their quiet march to the outpost, and Gwen glanced around at those who remained. Tylindra's group had seven people, and the other group had five. The large force soon melded into the shadows until Gwen couldn't see any of them. She watched and waited, anxiety making her legs tremor. She shifted from leg to leg, trying to dispel the shaking, but it didn't help.

"They've reached the doors," Tylindra said.

"How do you know?" Gwen asked.

"I can see them."

Gwen looked at the elf, awed. "Really?"

"Yes. We elves have excellent vision in the dark."

I need a rune that does that, Gwen thought.

"Prepare yourself," Tylindra said. "We move in—"

A horn blared in the distance, followed shortly after by cries of surprise.

"Onward!" Tylindra shouted.

Gwen ran ahead, following the others of her group. Tylindra led them forward, then branched to the left. The distance didn't seem far to Gwen, but as they reached what she guessed was the halfway point, she was already panting, both her legs and lungs on fire. She and two other people fell behind, but Tylindra and the rest barely seemed affected and quickly outdistanced them. By the time Gwen and her two companions reached the outpost, the others had already made it inside.

"Should we wait out here for them?" Gwen gasped.

The other two looked at each other and shook their heads, then entered into the doorway. Gwen waited by the door as she tried to catch her breath, constantly surveying her surroundings. It was quiet around her, but the sounds of battle echoed from the main building. Gwen stepped into the doorway and listened intently.

A metallic tapping noise caught her attention, but otherwise there was nothing. No screams, no one fighting. Curiosity convinced her to see what the noise was and she crept down a long narrow hall. Several doors lined each side, most of them open. Gwen glanced inside each one, but there was nothing of interest until she reached the last door before a stairwell.

The tapping noise came from within, and Gwen risked a look inside. A dwarf, one of her party members, was trying to break a lock on a wooden chest. He glanced up at her and offered a nod, then went back to his work. Footsteps reverberated from the stairwell, and Gwen saw Tylindra and the others coming down.

"There's no one in this building," she said. "We checked everything. A source told us there should have been soldiers in here."

"What does that mean?" Gwen asked.

"It might be a trap."

"I thought Roland said everyone had kept quiet?"

"As far as we know, they did. That doesn't mean there isn't a spy in our midst. We need to get to the others and make sure they aren't being overwhelmed."

Tylindra led the charge out into the small courtyard and across to the main building. Gwen spotted a few bodies on the ground, both soldiers and rebellion members. She didn't see Tobias among them and breathed a sigh of relief.

Something whizzed past Tylindra's head and Gwen stopped in her tracks as an arrow struck the ground a few feet away.

"Archers!" someone cried.

Gwen rushed into the building, pausing at the doorway. Blood covered the floor, and there were more bodies. She looked back and saw three members of the group get hit with multiple arrows and collapse, including the dwarf she'd seen trying to break the lock. Tylindra made a hasty charge inside, half dragging a wounded man. The last member, another human, stumbled in behind them.

"If they've got archers up top, there's no way we're getting out of here without heavy losses," the man said.

"We need to find a way up there," Tylindra said, setting the wounded man against the wall. "Gwen, I need you to stay here with Braeden. I'll be back as quickly as I can, but we've got to take care of those archers."

Gwen resisted the urge to panic. "I'm not a healer," she said.

"None of us are, but I can't carry him up the stairs with me. Just keep pressure on his wound until I get back. Can you do that?"

"Yes," Gwen answered.

"Good. Stay here."

Tylindra and the other human left. Gwen knelt beside Braeden and pushed her hand over the wound on his chest. A piece of a broken arrow shaft stuck out, and Gwen had to spread her fingers around it to put pressure on the wound. Blood seeped out anyway and coated her hand. Braeden groaned weakly, his eyes closed. Gwen swallowed hard, hoping the man didn't die, but the wound looked bad.

"Where are they?" she asked impatiently. The sounds of battle were getting less frequent and Gwen didn't know which side was winning. Braeden's body slumped a bit and went still, his chest no longer moving. Gwen removed her hand, wiping the blood onto his clothes. He was dead and she knew it.

She stood and went in the same direction Tylindra had gone. There were more lifeless bodies, and she stepped over them as she navigated her way along the hall. A hand grabbed onto her ankle and she screamed, jerking her foot away. It was a soldier. The man was surrounded by a growing pool of blood.

"Help," he rasped.

"Where's the prison?"

"Down b-below," he stuttered. "Please help me."

Gwen shook her head and backed away from him. Everything inside her screamed at her to help the man. She silenced the internal voice by imagining the soldier as the one responsible for torturing her father. The guilt lessened and she ran ahead. Gwen found stairs leading belowground and hurried down them.

She reached the bottom and rushed through the dimly lit tunnel, glancing into every cell. They were all empty. Gwen's heart began to pound in her chest. Had the soldier's killed them all? Her eyes welled with tears as she neared the end of the tunnel. There were only a few more cells left. Gwen heard a voice and paused. It sounded like …

"Tobias?" she called out.

"Gwen?"

Tobias stepped out from the last cell on the right and waved her forward. Gwen closed the distance and wrapped her arms around Tobias.

"Where's my father? Have you seen him?"

"He's in there," Tobias replied.

Gwen released him and hurried into the cell. Boris was lying on the ground covered in blood. Countless lash marks covered his flesh, but he was still alive.

"Father," Gwen said brokenly. She dropped to her knees, wanting to hold him but knowing it would cause him pain.

"Gwen," Boris whispered, his voice strained. "Closer."

Gwen leaned over her father, her eyes scanning his pain-filled face. "You're going to be all right," she said. Her tears spilled freely, some of them falling onto Boris's cheek. "We're going to get you out of here."

"No," Boris said. "I'm dying."

"Don't say that," Gwen sobbed.

"Listen to me …" Boris struggled to speak and

he fell silent for a moment. Gwen touched the side of his face, running her fingers along his wrinkled skin. "You're not my … real … daughter," he managed to say.

"What do you mean? You're all I've ever known."

"You were brought to us … a stranger left you …"

"Who?"

Boris tried to speak, but he coughed feebly and blood flecked his lips. "I … love …" His voice failed and his head lolled to the side. Gwen threw herself onto her father and sobbed. She didn't want to believe that he was dead and told herself over and over that he was going to hug her any minute, but he never did.

"I'm sorry, Gwen," Tobias said softly.

She sat up and spun her head around to look at him. "You're sorry? It's your fault he's dead! If you and Roland had gathered these people faster, we could have gotten here earlier!"

Tobias let her rage at him, his head lowered. Gwen got up and struck Tobias in the chest over and over. She was overcome with pain and pushed past him, rushing along the tunnel and back up the stairs. Gwen could hear Tobias following her, and she ran as fast as she could, not thinking about anything except escaping her grief. She entered the courtyard and kept running.

"Gwen!" Tobias shouted from behind her.

She turned around to unleash her anger at him again and spotted the shadowy silhouettes of archers on top of the outpost. The archers that she

had completely forgotten about in her anguish.
Time slowed.
There was a click.
A whizzing sound.
A wet thud.
Tobias dropped.
"No!" Gwen screamed.

CHAPTER 18

Conal

For two days, they traveled south through the mountainous dwarf kingdom. Conal teamed up with Bryok and Torgreth, leaving Voldar to travel with Drustan.

"They should get on well," Torgreth chuckled. "They're both grumps."

Before setting out on their journey, Conal had admired the walking staffs Bryok and Drustan had in hand. "Where did you find those?"

"Had these made some time ago," Bryok replied, holding out the smooth ebony staff crowed with a carved dragon's head, two emeralds set in place as the eyes. "Here." He handed the staff to Conal.

"By the gods," Conal sputtered, surprised at the near weightless heft to the staff. Yet the wood felt hard and dense. "What sort of wood is this?"

"It's called dragonwood," Drustan answered, shifting an irritated look at Bryok. "And before you ask, you can't find it anywhere anymore. When the dragons died out, so did their forests."

"But you said you knew –"

"We better get going," Bryok interrupted, shooting a 'keep-your-mouth-shut-about-dragons' look at him.

Giving Drustan and Voldar an hour head start, they had been careful to stifle the urge to catch up. They had eschewed horses as Voldar reminded them that, "Dwarves don't ride horses. We have ponies. And I don't know where we're gonna find dwarf ponies around here."

Though Conal had been through parts of the northern tips of the kingdom back in his highwayman days, he was impressed with the beautiful ruggedness of the land, the thickly forested mountains, the small villages of stone-hewn cottages, and the friendliness of the citizens. Even the border guards were friendly.

When they had approached the border station, Torgreth took the lead. "Let me do the talking."

While Bryok and Conal patiently waited by the border barrier, Torgreth ambled over to the two guards. Conal couldn't hear what was said, but saw the guards point at Torgreth and grin. After a bit of conversation, the barrier pole raised, and the travelers wished a good trip.

Once they were out of ear shot, Conal asked, "What did you say to them?"

Torgreth smirked and leaned over. "They're cousins of mine on my Mama's side. Pointed at my clothes and said it didn't matter what I wore, they knew who I was. Told me to be careful, 'cause they're still lookin' for me and Voldar. Said Voldar and Drustan were about an hour ahead of us. They'll keep good and quiet for us. They don't like what's been goin' on either."

That was two days ago. Since then, the trip had been remarkably uneventful. The inns had the usual one or two 'big people' rooms where the beds were larger, but the tables and chairs were lower and Conal felt like his knees were hitting his chest when he ate, though the ale was good.

They were an hour from Morendir when they met up with Drustan and Voldar waiting in a clump of trees by the road. The road curved around a low hill before opening up to a wide valley. In the distance, the city lay tucked against the mountains, a double gate in the middle of the tall sloping crenelated walls. Carved into the mountain behind the sprawling city was the citadel, the castle keep of the king of Gurim-duhr. Flanking the wide iron doors stood two granite statues twenty stories high of ancient warriors in helmet and armor, their hands resting on their swords.

"We need to find a place to stay," Drustan commented. "If the inn is still there, let's meet at the Stag and Boar."

"You been here before," Torgreth said, surprised.

"A long time ago."

"The inn's still there. It's a good choice, out of the way."

"Give us an hour head start," Drustan said.

Two hours later, Conal experienced the critical stare of the guards who studied him and Bryok with overt mistrust.

"What's yer business here?" one guard gruffly asked, ignoring Torgreth.

"Now just a minute you," Torgreth bowed up. "Since when do you harass folks that want to do business in our city?"

"Business? Bah. If yer merchants, where's yer stuff?" He abruptly frowned. "You look familiar."

"Well you don't," Torgreth retorted. "And who

said we were merchants? We're traders. Now can we be on our way?"

The guard hesitated then flipped a hand waving them through.

"That was quick thinking," Conal quietly complimented as they walked through the gates.

Torgreth chuckled. "First thing I could think of."

The dwarf led them through the crowded streets. Despite the obvious abundance of dwarves, there were enough humans and even a few elves among the cacophony that Conal's and Bryok's presence was not unusual though Conal noted the curious looks of some of the residents while others seemed quite indifferent.

Torgreth turned off to a side street well before the main market square. Another side street later and they stood under the hanging carved wooden sign of a stag and boar. Entering the inn, Conal glanced around the main room, seeing Drustan and Voldar seated in the corner.

"About time you got here," Voldar groused.

Conal had yet to pull the chair out when the inn's door opened and a dozen guards burst in. Catching sight of the new arrivals, they swarmed towards them.

"Hullo Voldar, Torgreth," the sergeant of the guard said with an arrogant grin. "Nice of you to come home. Who're yer friends." The sergeant was a stout dwarf with his dark brown beard done up on braids.

"Hullo Bagrun," Voldar sneered. "I see they let you outta yer cage again."

"Aren't you the comedian. You dressed fer a part in a play? Which part you playin', the whiny little girl or the idiot brother?"

"I tried out fer those parts, but they said you were playin' both. It was a stretch of actin', but they said you were perfect for the parts." He sipped his ale, his eyes locked on his adversary.

Several of the guards did their best to hide their smirks while Bagrun, unable to think of a repartee, pursed his lips.

"You been missed," Bagrun said, "and the king wants you back."

"You mean Havyrd wants us back."

"Don't matter who. You comin' peaceful?"

"What about my friends?"

"He wants to see them too."

"Why? They're not dwarves. They're just merchants."

Bagrun barked a laugh. "Merchants? You all better get your story straight."

"We're not here to cause trouble," Bryok placated, spreading his hands as if to show deference. "Of course we will come with you, Captain."

"Sergeant," Bagrun corrected though flattered.

"Ah, my apologies. I naturally assumed you were an officer as my experience in other kingdoms is that a king always sends a person of high rank when wishing to personally see someone. It is obvious the king must hold you in high regard."

"Yes, well, of course he holds me in high regard," he preened before casting a condescending eye on Voldar and Torgreth, "unlike someone else here who chose to tuck tail and run."

"Does it have to be right this minute?" Conal pleasantly asked, his plan to sneak into the citadel crumbling like a house of cards. "I haven't ordered yet."

"Yer drink can wait."

"C'mon," Voldar said with a longsuffering sigh, scooting his chair back and standing. "Let's get this over with before Bagrun says the king is gonna make him a general."

Bagrun led the way through the city, the group receiving a mixture of stares, some curious others more of a scowl at the king's guards who chose to ignore the deprecating looks.

Despite apprehension, Conal took in the surroundings, especially when they emerged from the city dwellings to the narrow bridge that crossed a deep chasm separating the citadel from the city. Built from the granite of the mountains, the bridge gently arced across the gorge ending at the wide portico that shielded the tall oak doors. He craned his head to gaze up at the twin statues, stained and darkened by the ravages of time.

"Step lively now," Bagrun commanded, leading them across the bridge.

Halfway across, Bryok covertly tapped Conal's hand. When Conal looked up at him, he placed something soft in Conal's hands. Conal glanced down at his cupped hand to see a clump of cotton. Puzzled, he shifted a glance back up to Bryok who, though focused to his front, tapped his ear several times as though brushing something away.

Understanding swept through Conal and he

slipped the cotton into his pocket.

Once through the doors, they stepped into an expansive foyer with a high ceiling supported by delicately carved columns left in place when the chamber had first been cut out. The granite floor, polished smooth from the centuries of foot traffic, glimmered in a dull patina.

Bagrun directed them through the foyer and into a wide hallway leading to an even wider set of grand stairs within a room so large Conal turned around to take it all in. The room rose four stories high with balconies and stairs and doors heading off in all directions.

Of a curious note was the eerie quiet, for no dwarves bustled about their various duties. No doors opened or closed; no dwarves swarmed the stairs or dawdled on the balconies. It was as if everyone had gone home leaving the room to whatever ghosts might linger.

"Awfully quiet in here," Conal commented.

"Shush," Bagrun reprimanded. "You are a guest here. Act like one."

"Guest? I was ordered here. I'd just as soon go back to the inn where I was enjoying myself."

Glaring at him, Bagrun picked up the pace as they marched up the stairs.

Another hallway met them at the top of the stairs. They were halfway down when Bagrun stopped.

"We're almost to the King's Hall. Here's the rules. When you step through the door, you will kneel, then walk to the middle of the king's chamber and kneel again. If King Rorkyn recognizes you, he will tell you to come forward. When Havyrd tells you to stop, you stop and kneel three times. You wait until the king speaks to you first. When you are allowed to speak, you will begin with the greeting of "Blessings and Peace upon you, Great King." You are to bow each time you are requested to speak. Do not avert your eyes, but look at him directly as an honest dwarf would."

"What?" Voldar exclaimed. "What kind of crap is this? Who came up with this garbage? Who's he think he is, some sort of god? I'm not gonna do all that nonsense." He defiantly folded his arms.

"Then you will be compelled to do it. You have no choice."

"I do have a choice," Voldar snapped. He turned around and started to walking back to the stairs before breaking into a run.

"Stop him," Bagrun ordered.

But it was too late. By the time the guards reacted, Voldar had sped away, taking four stairs at a time as he leaped down to the next floor. However, instead of heading for the main doors, Voldar led the guards on a wild chase through the citadel.

With half his troop chasing Voldar, Bagrun's smugness began to evaporate. Praying that Voldar would be quickly cornered and brought back, his patience frayed the longer they waited. Deciding he better get the others into see the king before they too made a run for it, he ordered the group to move on, silently rehearsing his excuse when they entered the king's chambers.

Looking up at the two druids, he said, "You two

need to leave your staffs outside."

Bryok placed a gentle hand on Bagrun's arm, fixing him with an intent stare. "You want us to take our staffs with us. We're just old men and you know we need them."

Bagrun blinked as he stared back at Bryok, surprised he hadn't noticed how decrepit the man was. He shifted a look at Drustan, noting the same aged frailty. "Yes, yes, of course you may take your staffs with you."

"Thank you."

Conal frowned at Bryok who held a finger to his lips then pointed to a rune on his arm.

At the end of the hall, two guards lounged next to the doors of the king's chamber, chatting amiably though obviously bored. Unaffected by the approaching group, they languorously reached to open the doors, one guard stifling a yawn.

"Wake up you two," Bagrun growled.

Ignoring him, they swung the doors open, waited for the last dwarf to enter then closed the doors behind them and resumed their desultory dialogue.

The room was not as large or grand as Conal expected. Lit by too few sconces and candelabra, the room felt dull mixed with a heavy lethargy. Bored guards sat on both sides of the doors, quietly talking amongst themselves. With a passing glance at the visitors, they returned to their conversations.

What Conal could see was a room with a high ceiling supported by columns. Sconces attached to the columns provided a row of lights leading to a throne set on a platform, the rest of the room fading into shadows.

Rorkyn sat on the throne, an overly large high-back chair draped with animal pelts, his feet barely touching the floor. The brooding face, wrinkled with age, stared vacantly at the floor, his white beard flat across his protruding belly. The hairline had receded so that only the back and sides of his head sprouted close cropped white hair. Beneath the woolen mantel, a shirt of chainmail glimmered in the reflected light. The once powerful arms that had wielded a stout double-bladed axe in battle had grown soft. The sword he usually held in his hands now leaned against the side of the throne. Glancing up when the door opened, he readjusted his crown and beckoned them forward.

"Remember to bow," Bagrun stage-whispered, leading them to the middle of the room and stopping.

Having forgotten when, where and the number of times to bow, Conal waited to take his que from the dwarves who were themselves confused for some bowed while others kneeled. Seeing their comrades in different poses caused them to adjust resulting in something that imitated the bobbing ponies on a merry-go-round.

"Damn it all," Rorkyn barked. "Just stand still." Glaring at the visitors, his thick brows furrowed, he scratched his cheek through the grey flecked auburn beard. "You," he snarled at Bagrun. "Where's the other dwarf? And who are these men?"

Bagrun swallowed hard. "Uh, well, your Majesty, uh… it seems that, what I mean to say is that, while I had the two brothers as you requested, one of them escaped, leaped right away, he did, before I could stop him."

"Your Majesty," a warm voice cooed, interrupting the interrogation. Out of the shadows, Havyrd edged up the stairs to stand next to the king.

Conal felt a sudden tranquility flush through him and he smiled as he relaxed and studied the advisor to the dwarf king. Watching Havyrd lean in and whisper in the king's ear, Conal was surprised at how short the man was, probably no taller than the dwarf he advised. Unlike the brawn of a dwarf, Havyrd was thin and pale, like one who feared the sun. His thin unwashed black hair hung in strands down to his shoulders. He wore the robe of a wizard with loose cowl and draping sleeves. Conal's peace was momentarily broken when Havyrd turned to smile at him, his teeth root stained.

Havyrd swiveled his bony face back to the king. "My Lord, are we not absent a dwarf, the very one causing us the most trouble?" When he spoke, the room filled with a sweet calmness infused with lethargy, and an overwhelming urge to float in serenity.

Conal felt Bryok nudge him and shot a quick glance to see him rub his ear. Taking the hint, Conal separated a piece of the cotton and, pretending to scratch his ear, stuffed the wadding into hole. He paused plugging the other ear when he noticed Havyrd shifting his gaze towards him.

"Where is Voldar?" the king demanded, glaring at Torgreth.

"Don't know," he shrugged. "Could be anywhere."

"Why did they flee?" Havyrd coached.

"Yes," the Rorkyn nodded. "Why did you flee?"

"Didn't like making witchcraft spells for him," Torgreth answered, beginning to slur his words.

Avoiding the subject, Havyrd leaned in to Rorkyn. "Who did he bring here with him? Are they spies? Have Voldar and Torgreth turned against you? Are these men really assassins come to kill you?"

"We are simple merchants looking to trade," Bryok spoke.

Conal struggled to place the other wadding in his ear as though some terrible force clamped his body in place. Straining against the force, he bent his head down closer to his hand just in time to hear Torgreth's detached voice say,

"They are not merchants. They are assassins come to kill you."

CHAPTER 19

Gwen

Something inside Gwen snapped.

She felt the pulse of the magic and threw herself fully into it. Power coursed through every inch of her, welling internally with nowhere to go. Gwen screamed in pain and fell to her knees. Her flesh burned, and sweat collected on her forehead. She recalled the name of the lightning rune and said, "*Tintreach*."

A jagged bolt of lightning arced from her hand, snaking its way through the dark sky and striking the soldiers atop the outpost. Their dying screams were like fuel to the fire burning within her. She spoke the rune again and again, blasting the front of the fortress until the stones cracked and sent fragments airborne.

People escaped the building, running and ducking for cover. Gwen didn't know if they were friend or foe, and she didn't care either. She just kept hurling lightning at the outpost as she slowly rose back to her feet. Tobias hadn't moved yet. In any other circumstance, Gwen would have panicked. In her current state, her sole focus was on the power flowing through her. She was like a conduit, allowing the raw force of nature to channel through her body.

Gwen saw a flash, then a sphere of steadily glowing light formed around a group of people exiting the outpost. Aimil was shielding them from the lightning. One of Gwen's bolts struck the shield and bounced off, ricocheting into the doorway of the outpost. The stones of the upper portion gave way and the entrance caved in.

Destruction was everywhere, but Gwen wasn't satisfied. She stalked forward and stood guard over Tobias as she blasted away at the outpost. The people who had fled were no longer in the way, and she unleashed even more rage. The magic was taking every ounce of strength she had. She was aware that she had lost control. That meant nothing to her. Someone was shouting her name, but she ignored their calls.

Gwen's legs trembled and her focus was fading. Darkness was creeping toward her, bidding her to enter its embrace. She wanted to slip into the darkness, to lose herself completely and never feel pain anymore.

But it was a lie.

The darkness didn't want to comfort her. It wanted to suffocate her. Gwen pushed the exhaustion away and regained control, then cut ties with her connection to the magic. Her strength was gone, and she collapsed beside Tobias. She wanted to check his wound, but she couldn't move and her eyes wouldn't focus. They were dry and her eyelids were heavy. Gwen called his name, but she couldn't hear her own voice over the ringing in her ears.

Her struggle to keep the darkness at bay became a losing battle. She closed her eyes and sailed away into oblivion.

When Gwen awoke, light was shining through the fabric of her tent. She was on her side and laid there for a long while, trying to remember where she was and how she had gotten there. Her memories were disjointed and the pounding in her skull didn't help. A shuffling noise at her side startled her and she rolled over to see Aimil sitting cross-legged.

"You're alive," Aimil said. Gwen couldn't tell if she was being sarcastic or not.

"Should I be dead?" Her voice was coarse and sounded like someone else's.

"With what I saw last night, I'm surprised you aren't. You lost control over the magic and nearly killed innocent people. I warned you about losing control."

"I don't remember much," Gwen said guiltily. "What happened?"

Aimil picked up a wooden bowl and handed it to Gwen. It contained water and Gwen sat up to drink from it. The liquid was cool and eased the ache in her throat, but the movement increased the pounding in her head.

"You demolished the outpost," Aimil said. "And a lot of other things. It's a good thing you went unconscious. You might have died otherwise."

"What about the prisoners? Are they safe?"

"A lot of them were already dead or dying. We didn't save many of them, but this wasn't just about them. This was a message to Torian. The people have had enough and are going to fight back. We slaughtered all but two soldiers."

"Why?" Gwen wanted them all dead.

"If there was no one to run to the king and tell him what happened, then what good would ransacking the outpost have done? They serve as our messengers."

Gwen drank the rest of the water and laid back down. Her headache eased a little, but not much. "I feel like my head is going to split open," she complained.

"Accept it as a lesson learned," Aimil said. "Never use magic when your emotions are in turmoil."

"I don't plan to do that again."

"Good." Aimil stood and pushed the tent flaps open, then paused and looked back at Gwen. "Despite our victory, we lost many. Roland has the others packing up, but you should stay in here and get some rest. I'll come back when they are ready to break down your tent."

Aimil left, and Gwen stared up at the tent's ceiling. She remembered vividly that her father had died, but everything else was a blur. Her eyes welled with tears. She didn't think their outcome was much of a victory. And then she remembered what Boris had told her, that he wasn't her father. Eradore and Tobias had been right.

Tobias.

Gwen sat up too quickly and immediately regretted it. The world spun around her and she became disoriented, but she managed to crawl outside of the tent before she retched. The dizziness faded and Gwen found enough strength to stand and survey the area.

Roughly half of the camp had been broken down already, and the rebellion members had commandeered two wagons that had been outside the outpost's stable. One of them was filled with bodies. Gwen shuffled toward it but was intercepted by Roland.

"You shouldn't be moving around," he said. His tone was authoritative, but the look on his face was one of concern. "How are you feeling?"

"Like I was hit by a boulder."

"Would you like me to help you back to your tent?"

"No, I can manage," Gwen replied. "Where's Tobias?"

It was only there for a brief moment, but the pained expression that crossed over his face said everything. Gwen's legs gave out, and she crumpled to the ground. She wanted to cry, but no tears flowed. Roland knelt and picked her up, then carried her back to her tent. He set her down gently and heaved a sigh.

"I'm sorry. I know Tobias was your friend. He was mine, too. The world has lost a good man. We're taking our fallen with us to ensure they receive a proper burial." He paused. "If you need anything, let me know."

Roland left her alone. She didn't want to believe that Tobias was dead. As the realization set in, she blamed herself. If she hadn't been so insistent on rescuing her father, then he'd still be alive. This time the tears did come. She had failed to save her father. Tobias was dead. What did she have now?

When Aimil eventually returned, Gwen had barely moved. She hadn't slept either, but merely stared off at nothing.

"It's time," Aimil said.

Gwen got up and followed her in silence. They left the tent and Aimil made Gwen grab some bread and an apple, then watched her eat it.

"Loss is never easy," Aimil said, climbing onto a large black horse. Gwen mounted the horse beside her, a smaller speckled gelding. The animal was docile and began a steady trot at Gwen's flick of the reigns. The two rode together without speaking, leaving the others behind. Gwen wondered why they were leaving without them, but assumed they would catch up.

The silence became too much and Gwen said, "I feel like it's my fault."

"That's a natural response," Aimil said. "But you are not to blame. Tobias would have gone to the outpost and fought whether you were involved or not."

"I don't think so. If my father hadn't been taken, Tobias wouldn't have had any reason to be there."

"Whether it was this outpost or another, this battle was going to happen regardless. Trust me, there is nothing to gain by blaming yourself. It won't bring the dead back and it won't make you feel any better."

Aimil spoke so matter-of-factly that Gwen decided it was impossible to argue with the woman. She considered Boris's last words again. If he wasn't her father, who was? And who was her mother?

"You said before there was a place where a mage could learn their true name," Gwen said. "Have you been there before?"

"Yes, a few times. Why do you ask?"

"I need to know who I really am," Gwen replied. "My father confirmed what Eradore told me, but he died before he could say who brought me to him."

"There's a mage I know in Steepcross who could give you a rune. She's a little … eccentric, but she's harmless. She has many runes you could choose from."

"As many as you?"

"No," Aimil replied. "There are few like me. At least, I've only encountered a few. There may be others, but I have only traveled among the human kingdoms."

"I've never traveled anywhere," Gwen said. "Is the trip dangerous?"

Aimil turned to look at her. "There is little danger, but it's a long journey. On a quick horse with minimal stops, it could take a few days. The place is on the border of Steepcross and Auleavell, the elven kingdom."

"I want to go," Gwen said. "Will you come with me?"

"I think I can do that," Aimil said, offering a smile. "Who knows, maybe I'll find another rune while we're there."

The two stopped to rest and stretch their legs, allowing the horses to graze near a stream. The rest of the rebellion members caught up to them, and they traveled as a group back to the city of Penshaw. Gwen tried not to think about the horrible events of the night before, turning her thoughts instead to the future.

When they reached Penshaw, Gwen and Aimil

returned to Eradore's tower. Aimil relayed the events to Eradore while Gwen sat quietly. Although they had just arrived, Gwen was ready to go. She wanted to find out where her real parents were and why they had left her to be cared for by someone else.

"This minor victory came with a great cost. I'm afraid it may have set us back further than any of us anticipated," Eradore said. "Even so, we will continue to undermine the king and his rule."

"As we should," Aimil said. "Gwen and I are going to Steepcross. She wants to know her true name."

Eradore frowned. "I assumed she would, but not so quickly. Are you sure this is what you want to do?"

"It's not about what I want to do, it's about what I *need* to do," Gwen replied.

"Very well. No one will stop you, of course. You are free to do as you wish, but I would ask a favor of you."

"What is it?"

"I need a message delivered to a friend in Auleavell. I don't trust anyone else to do it, and magical means are … not the best option right now."

"Who am I taking it to?"

"Her name is Lyra and she is an ally of the rebellion. She's trying to drum up support within the court of Auleavell, but it's not easy. Auleavell's king, Falael, wants nothing to do with our struggles."

"He's a coward," Aimil said.

"That remains to be seen," Eradore replied. "There are rumors that Torian wants to expand his kingdom. If it comes to war, Falael will have no other option but to fight. Lyra is trying to convince him of that. This letter will help her argument."

Eradore handed Gwen a scrollcase. She took it and held onto it tightly. "I'll deliver it to her as soon as I'm done in Steepcross."

"Thank you. I know you must have a lot on your mind, and I admire your tenacity to continue onward through the pain and the grief."

Gwen offered a nod.

"Let's get on with it, then," Aimil said. "We'll see you when we return, old friend."

Eradore smiled and escorted them out of the tower. Aimil led Gwen back to the stable they had boarded their horses at and retrieved them, then went to the market to get supplies. Aimil purchased everything they needed, then they left Penshaw behind, traveling east toward Steepcross.

Everything Gwen knew had only been a half-truth. There were so many uncertainties ahead, but Gwen was ready to face them.

She was finally going to learn who she really was.

CHAPTER 20

Conal

"Guards!" the king roared, leaning forward and thrusting a finger at Conal and the others. "Throw them in the dungeon."

Conal was the first to react, whirling around and yanking the sword out from Bagrun's scabbard. Bryok and Drustan followed suit, using their staffs to whack the nearby guards so hard as to knock them sprawling to the floor

Startled, Havyrd tried to regain control, using his most persuasive voice until he saw Conal advancing towards him. "You will put down your sword. Put down your sword." Fear exploded in his eyes when Conal failed to respond to his commands. Back-peddling away from the king, he shouted, "Kill them!" before spinning around and racing away.

But Conal intercepted him before he reached the door, spreading himself across the doorway.

Shocked at the man's speed, Havyrd jerked his arms out to his front, his hands as though reaching for Conal's throat as he voiced an incantation. "You cannot breathe. Your throat tightens. You are choking."

Impervious to his conjuring, Conal raised his sword causing Havyrd to flinch, only to have his stroke blocked by Torgreth who had somehow managed to find a sword of his own.

"What are you doing?" Conal flared, suddenly

defending himself against Torgreth's attack.

"That's right," Havyrd cried out. "You must protect me. Kill him."

"Protect Havyrd. Kill him," Torgreth intoned, pressing the attack.

While Conal deftly avoided Torgreth's blows, a panicked Havyrd sped back to the king, a terrible foreboding pulsing within that he was losing control.

The druids, doing their best to avoid killing or maiming the guards, had managed to corral them to a far corner.

"Get more guards," Havyrd shouted when the doors opened and Voldar marched in surrounded by the other half of Bagrun's troop.

Immediately understanding the discord, Voldar broke free and made a beeline towards Torgreth only to be slowed down when Havyrd intervened.

"Kill the intruders. Protect me."

Voldar jerked to a stop, confusion clouding his senses.

Seeing Voldar stop, Conal knew the reason. "Don't listen to him, Voldar," he cried out, parrying Torgreth's attack.

But it was too late as Havyrd's power swept through the dwarf and he looked around for a sword as the remaining guard members attacked the two druids.

"We need to get out of here, Sire," Havyrd urged, grabbing the aging king's arm.

"What's going on?" he growled as though suddenly aware of the fray.

"Assassins, Sire," Havyrd pressed, tugging the

king's arm. "We got to go."

"What?" Rorkyn thundered. "You think me coward that I cannot defend myself!" It was then he saw Voldar reaching for his sword. "What are you doing? Get away from my sword."

"Must protect Havyrd," Voldar chanted, wrapping his fingers around the hilt.

"Dammit you," Rorkyn barked. "Let go my sword." He grabbed Voldar's hand.

Refusing to let go, Voldar and Rorkyn struggled over the sword, both trying to pry the other's hands from the grip.

Havyrd frantically scanned the room. His hopes rose as he saw the guards swarming around the two tall men. Over by the door, the younger man was fending off Torgreth and two guards. Standing to full height, he held his arms up and spoke in the most entrancing voice he could muster.

"Listen to me. Stop. Put down your weapons."

The effect was instant and the dwarves immediately dropped their swords to their sides. The two druids, staffs held at the ready, likewise paused, warily regarding the dwarves surrounding them.

His confidence returning, Havyrd cast a haughty glare at the druids when out the corner of his eye he saw movement. His head jerked to the right to see the young man leaping towards him, sword raised.

Though surprised at the sudden lull, Conal reacted with speed, his body moving without thinking as he slipped past Torgreth and the two guards. He was upon Havyrd before the man had a chance to defend himself. The last thing Conal saw was the abject terror in the man's eyes as his arms moved up to block the blow.

In a blinding swift arc, Conal's blade swung down with such force, it sliced through the man's neck. The head momentarily wobbled before flipping down to the floor, blood spurting out the neck as the body crumbled to the ground.

It wasn't until he stood over the decapitated body that the enormity of his act burst within, for he had finally killed a man. The first impulse was to retch. It wasn't that he hadn't seen men killed before. It's just that someone else was always responsible.

Fighting back the taste of bile, he flicked his head around to see the startled dwarven faces when a faint burst of reddish light filled the room for an instant then vanished.

The king was the first to speak. "What goes on here?" His thick brows furrowed in a deep 'V'. He stared down at the headless body of his former confidant and the pool of blood creeping around the still warm flesh. He blinked in lucid understanding.

He snapped his head up to give Conal a hard stare. "Did you do this?"

Realizing the king had spoken to him, Conal stood to full height and pulled the cotton form his ears. "Sire?"

"I said, 'Did you do this?'"

"Yes, Sire."

Rorkyn's attention abruptly shifted to the gloom of the room. "Why is it so dark in here?"

"That is the way he wanted it, Sire," Bagrun replied, flicking his hand at a guard to light more sconces.

As the room filed with light, the king returned his focus on Conal then the two druids. "Who are you?"

"I am Conal, Sire." He respectfully bowed.

"Why did you kill him?"

"He was evil, Sire."

Rorkyn's face scrunched as he struggled to remember, snippets of the past year gaining clarity. "Why was he evil?"

"He had the magic of the Rune Tongue, King Rorkyn," Bryok answered.

Rorkyn shifted his gaze to discover who spoke, seeing Voldar and Torgreth standing to the side. "You two! You ran away from here."

"Yes, Sire," Voldar boldly replied, stepping forward. "We ran because no one would do anything about him." He jabbed a finger at the crumpled corpse. Seeing the king returning to himself again, Voldar unbridled his tongue. "He had power over you. You did everything he wanted you to do. The kingdom is falling apart and all you did was sit on the throne and let Havyrd rule. He was destroying everything. Instead of mining and building like any respectable dwarf would do, he had us carving runes into bones."

As his memory crystalized, Rorkyn twisted his head to level a stare at the two druids. "Who are you?"

"I am Drustan, Sire." He bowed. "And this is my brother Bryok. We are half-druids." Seeing Rorkyn's stiffen, he hastily added, "We are not here to harm you. In fact, we are here to seek your help."

"Help?" Rorkyn placed a hand under his chin and twisted his head, cracking his neck before staring at Bagrun. "Get me something to drink… an ale."

"Yes, Sire," he replied before pointing a finger at a guard. "Get the king an ale."

"Where are all your servants, Sire?" Bryok asked, noting the absence of anyone except the guards.

"Don't need servants," he gruffly answered. "At least, I don't think I do… do I?" The last was directed at Bagrun.

"No, Sire. We're dwarves, remember? We don't have servants."

"Of course I remember," he growled. "I'm a dwarf, dammit." His attention snapped back to Drustan. "Help with what?"

Wondering if Havyrd's spell still lingered in the old man, Drustan explained, "Your advisor was a servant of Grimmar the Mage Breaker, advisor to the king of Isentol."

"Torian?" he barked. "That man has the gall to send someone to infiltrate my court?" He pushed himself to standing, wobbling a bit before demanding, "Where's my ale?"

The doors burst open and the guard returned with a pitcher of ale and an artfully carved pewter stein. "It's coming, Sire." With the help of another guard, he filled the stein and handed it to Bagrun who handed it to the king.

Rorkyn downed the entire contents in four swallows, smacking his lips. "Ah, Now I can think. Alright druid, speak. What is it you want?"

"Torian gains power, even as we speak. His army grows as does the strength of his magical arts."

"He's a magician, a wizard?" Rorkyn frowned, holding out the stein for a refill.

"No. He's gathered wizards and sorcerers and mages to his court. Their numbers grow daily."

With each passing minute, Rorkyn's clarity improved and he blinked in understanding. "The man has been raiding my northern frontier for the past several months… and I've done nothing about it." He cast a disgusted look at Havyrd's corpse. "Now I understand why."

"We are racing to get the surrounding kingdoms to join together to stop him," Bryok said. "Will you join us?"

"Who is 'we'?"

"Already rebellion occurs near in and around Isentol. Rhonyn awaits in your north."

"Who is he?" Rorkyn sat and leaned forward, forearms on his thighs

"He is a friend who owes allegiance to no man or dwarf."

"Or elf?"

"Or elf," Bryok agreed. "He comes when he's needed and right now, he knows he's needed."

"He has an army?" Rorkyn leaned back and scratched his cheek.

"His army is small, but elite."

Rorkyn paused to think. "That's it? That's all you got?"

"Sire," Drustan patiently explained. "We don't know who else has agreed. Like us, our friends have spread through the kingdoms garnering support. We don't know who else has agreed."

"But we do know," Bryok interrupted, "that if nothing is done, this kingdom will fall to Torian, just like all the others."

Rorkyn pursed his lips, his head bobbing in a slow nod. Conal again caught his attention. "Who are you?"

Conal sucked in a slow breath of irritation, and repeated, "I am Conal, Sire."

"Are you a druid?"

"No, Sire."

His stare narrowed when he saw the rune markings on Conal's arm. "Then who and what are you?"

Deciding to keep his newly discovered heritage to himself for the moment, Conal opened his shirt and pulled it back to reveal the tattoo. "I'm a Cobra."

Rorkyn jerked back while the other dwarves stutter-stepped away in fear.

"Assassin." Rorkyn gripped the arms of the throne chair.

"Yes." Conal strutted to stand before the king. "But have no fear, Great King. My quest is to restore the Kingdom of Isentol to the House of Kamron."

Though flattered to be called 'Great King,' Rorkyn cocked his head to the side. "Thought the House of Kamron died when he did."

"It is rumored his children still live," Bryok said, shooting Conal an irritated look.

"We're wasting precious time," Drustan

interrupted. "We need an answer. Will you help or not?"

"Forgive my impetuous brother, Sire." Bryok smoothly said, cocking an eyebrow at Drustan. "Yet he does have a point. Time is critical."

"Let me think about it," Rorkyn hesitated.

Before Bryok could entreat him further, Drustan said, "You have a bone room?"

"A what?"

"Yes," Bagrun answered for him, stepping up. "Havyrd had us carve runes into all sorts of bones then kept them in a room that only he had the key for."

Torgreth bent down and patted Havyrd's headless body, eventually turning him over. "Here it is." He lifted the key attached to a chain around the neck, wiping the blood off on Havyrd's robe.

"Where is the room?" Drustan asked.

"We know where it is," Voldar answered.

"Sire." Bryok's voice rose in volume. "The rune bones are dangerous. They need to be destroyed."

"But not by just anyone," Drustan joined in.

"You mispronounce the rune and you're dead," Conal added. "One can only imagine what Havyrd had in mind when he had these made." Conal hadn't a clue what he was talking about, but he figured if he sounded ominous enough, he'd be helping the two druids.

"What do you suggest we do with them," Rorkyn asked, assuming a regal air.

"With your permission," Bryok replied, "we will take them with us, away from the kingdom"

"Why?" Rorkyn said, suddenly suspicious. "We

have mages and wizards here in Gurim-duhr. Perhaps they ought to look at them first."

"If you so wish, Sire. But remember, Havyrd was Grimmar's man. Grimmar pretends to hate magic when, in fact, he is merely eliminating the competition, keeping those loyal only to him."

"Do you trust all your wizards and mages?" Conal asked. "Be a pity if one or more turned on you and you'd be right back where you were with Havyrd."

Rorkyn snarled at the thought. "Fine. Do what you want with them. Just get them out of here."

"Thank you, Sire." Bryok bowed.

"Will you fight with us?" Drustan challenged.

Rorkyn scrunched his face and stared at Bagrun. "Where're all my generals?"

"Spread throughout the kingdom, Sire, far away from here," Bagrun boldly answered. " Havyrd didn't want anyone around who might sway his control over you, so he had you order them to patrol the kingdom."

"Who's in command around here?"

Bagrun thought for a moment. "I guess I am, Sire."

"What rank do you hold?"

"I'm a sergeant, Sire."

"A sergeant?" Rorkyn sputtered. "That fool entrusted my safety to a mere sergeant? That's irresponsible. I can't allow that. You are promoted to captain. Find someone to replace you."

Bagrun's initial annoyance at the 'mere sergeant' comment morphed to surprise at the sudden promotion to captain, skipping over lieutenant. "Yes, Sire."

"What's your recommendation, captain?"

Bagrun closed his mouth and rapidly thought about the past year before saying, "Go for it, Sire. Be the first one to join, if that's the case. Let no one say that a dwarf wasn't at the front, leading the way."

"Well spoken, Captain." Rorkyn turned to Bryok. "You have my answer."

"Thank you, Sire"

"The bone room?" Drustan urged.

"Go." Rorkyn flipped a hand at them, shooing them away. "You go with them, Captain Bagrun."

"Yes, Sire."

Voldar led the way to a room close by, adjacent to Havyrd's quarters, inserting the key into the padlock and opening the door.

The room was the size of a large walk-in closet, filled with crates of rune bones stacked on top of each other. Bryok and Drustan shared an apprehensive glance then walked in. Selecting a bone from an open crate, Drustan was the first to react.

"I hope we're not too late." He flipped it over to show Bryok then flung the bone back into the box.

Bryok selected another bone and turned it for Drustan to see.

The half-druid's head shot up to gape at his brother. "This does not bode well."

"What?" Conal asked, not sure he wanted to hear the answer.

Ignoring him, Drustan turned to Bagrun. "How often did Havyrd send the bones north?"

Bagrun swallowed hard. "Every couple of weeks, protected by dwarves until they got to the border. Then the man-guards took over. We haven't sent a shipment since Voldar and Torgreth took off."

"How long is that?"

"About a month," Voldar answered.

Bryok studied the number of boxes in the room. "Looks like he was keeping back quite a bit. Why?"

"What's on the bones?" Conal demanded.

"Incantations," Drustan replied.

"I know that," Conal huffed. "What kind of incantations?"

Instead of answering, Drustan turned to Bagrun, desperation in his voice. "We need to get these out of here, now. We need a wagon. We also need all these crates nailed shut."

As Bagrun whirled around to issue orders, Drustan leaned in towards Bryok. "We need to split up. I'll take the bones back to our place. You and Conal head back to Tir Manach."

"Why?" Conal interrupted.

"Because King Caldyr needs persuasion and you're the man to do it."

"Me?" Conal squeaked. "Why would he listen to me?"

"Because Lord Pharyl is favorably inclined to you," Bryok answered.

"Yeah, but he's not the king," Conal argued.

"He's close enough," Drustan firmly stated. "Bryok will go with you to protect you."

"How about a dwarf?" Torgreth interrupted, causing the three men to twist their heads to frown at him. "What I mean is that I can help persuade King Caldyr. Tell him that Rorkyn is already assembling the dwarf armies."

Drustan nodded. "Good idea." Addressing Bryok, he said, "Once I get the bones safely away, I'll head up north to connect with Rhonyn. Meet me there."

Conal listened as Drustan gave further instructions. A thought popped into his head. *Wonder if we might bump into Oscon. Wouldn't that be sweet. I'd teach him a lesson he'd never forget.*

'Wake up, Conal," Bryok chastised. "We need to go. And you need to forget about Oscon."

Conal's eyes popped wide. "How'd you know what I was thinking?"

"I'm a half-druid, remember?" Bryok answered with a smile. "Besides, we don't have time to deal with the little fish."

"Little fish?" Conal scrunched a face in confusion.

"Didn't you know?"

"Know what?"

"About Oscon."

"What about him?"

Bryok studied him for a moment, realizing Conal had no clue. "Oscon is Caldyr's man, reporting back to him about what's going on in the kingdom."

"You mean…" Conal's jaw dropped.

Bryok chuckled. "Yes. The entire time you thought yourself a highwayman, you've been working for the king." Letting Conal stew for only a moment, he added, "But Oscon serves two masters.

All the reports he sent back were conveniently intercepted by another whose master lives in Havengarde."

Conal's jaw tightened. He'd been played the fool more than once. It was time to become the Cobra he was destined to be.

THE END OF BOOK ONE

ABOUT THE AUTHORS

Richard Fierce

Hey there!

I write fantasy and space opera, and you can find all my books in many different eBook stores. You can check out my website for more information about my books, my next projects, and events I'll be attending where you can meet me and even get signed books.

WEBSITE

www.richardfierce.com

pdmac

pdmac spent a career in the US Army before transitioning to education as a university Academic Dean. He transitioned again and now writes fulltime. He has a MA in Creative Writing and a Ph.D. in Theology. He is a member of the Blue Ridge Writers Guild, the Steampunk Writers and Artists Guild, and the Georgia Writers Association. A diverse author, writer, and editor, he has also edited a Literature anthology, served as managing editor of an archaeology magazine, ghost-written an autobiography, and has had poems, short stories, articles, and editorials published in various literary journals, magazines and newspapers. His most recent short stories appear in the *Short Story America* anthologies III and IV, *Poets in Hell*, *The Mulberry Fork Review*, and the Fantasy Anthology *Chronicles of Mirstone*. He has also sung back-up for Broadway plays, provided voice for radio plays, and acted and directed theater stage productions. In his off time, he and his wife race mountain bikes, kayak, and occasionally backpack sections of the Appalachian Trail. Additionally, he and his wife love to travel, their favorite place so far being Crete, Greece.

www.ingramcontent.com/pod-product-compliance
Lightning Source LLC
Chambersburg PA
CBHW050355190726
48284CB00007BB/2299